ANTIQUE SECRETS

A LOCUST POINT MYSTERY

LIBBY HOWARD

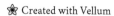 Created with Vellum

Stevens Family

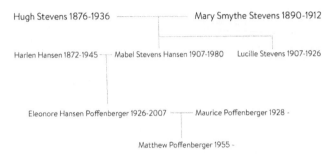

Hugh Stevens 1876-1936 ———————— Mary Smythe Stevens 1890-1912

Harlen Hansen 1872-1945 ——— Mabel Stevens Hansen 1907-1980   Lucille Stevens 1907-1926

Eleonore Hansen Poffenberger 1926-2007 ——— Maurice Poffenberger 1928 -

Matthew Poffenberger 1955 -

Hostenfelder Family

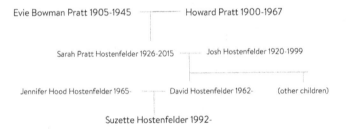

Evie Bowman Pratt 1905-1945 ——— Howard Pratt 1900-1967

Sarah Pratt Hostenfelder 1926-2015 ——— Josh Hostenfelder 1920-1999

Jennifer Hood Hostenfelder 1965- ——— David Hostenfelder 1962-   (other children)

Suzette Hostenfelder 1992-

"*M*iss Kay, I won! I won!" Henry jumped up and down, nearly whacking me in the head with the paddle he was waving around. Number fifty-two. And according to the auctioneer, my thirteen-year-old friend had just purchased a battered entertainment console from the sixties for the sweet price of thirty dollars. His father had given him forty and told him sternly to spend it wisely. I wasn't sure Judge Beck would consider this to be a wise investment, but I was glad that he decided to let Henry explore his love of antiquities with as little regulation as possible.

The boy had been so excited once he'd learned I was going to an auction, and had begged to come along. With his father's approval and my promise to not allow him to bring home anything too ridiculous, he'd been allowed to attend. I was grateful for his company as I was carefully deciding where to spend the earnings from the sale of various junk in my attic. The money from the ugly pitcher went to pay the hot tub bill, but I managed to pull together another three hundred from different odds and ends and decided to splurge and pick up something special for the house.

It *was* exciting, but my chest still felt heavy at the reminder of other estate sales I'd attended in the past. Eli and I used to haunt the auctions and flea markets, buying antiques and refurbished building materials. Early on, we'd been fixing up the dilapidated Victorian house, and searching for leaded windows and both interior and exterior trim. Later, we'd picked up lighting fixtures, parts to repair the dumbwaiter, and nice little touches that made our home an eclectic mix of antiques from the last century, with modern conveniences tastefully added in. He would have loved this. He would have been just as excited over our purchases as Henry was with his entertainment console.

"Miss Kay, Miss Kay," Henry hissed, elbowing me in the side. The fine art of casual ennui that was necessary to assume at an auction had completely escaped him.

I may have looked uninterested, but I was just as thrilled as he was, because coming up next to auction was the piece I was here to buy. It was, according to the auction tag, an inlaid mahogany Sheraton sideboard from the late nineteenth century. It was the reason that I'd borrowed Suzette's pick-up for this auction. Given that I would also be carting home an entertainment console, I was especially glad I'd brought the truck instead of my little sedan.

The bidding started at one fifty and I choked back a gasp. I should have known. After Henry had seen my interest in the piece, he'd busily searched the internet on his phone, whispering to me that it might go as high as three thousand. I only had three hundred. And if bidding started at one fifty, then there was a good chance we'd end far higher than my budget. I'd go home empty-handed; well, empty-handed except for Henry's entertainment console.

I steadied my breathing and tried for my best bored

expression while Henry nearly hyperventilated by my side. Oddly enough, no one bid at one fifty and the auctioneer dropped the starting bid to one hundred. Then to seventy-five. Then asked for an offer. I waited, because as Eli and I had learned, it's never good to be the first one to bid.

"Forty," a short, round bald man called out, raising his paddle.

The auctioneer rolled his eyes, then asked for forty-five. I hesitated until the last moment, then raised my paddle. Short, round bald man and I went back and forth until we reached one hundred, then two more joined in. Most times auctioneers ask other bidders to wait until one of the two active bidders dropped off, but this one seemed okay with managing four ongoing bidders.

Short, round bald man dropped off at two hundred, leaving me to duke it out with Soccer Mom and Metrosexual Man. At two fifty, it was just me and Metrosexual Man. I'd been delaying my bids, shaking my head and eyeing the sideboard as if assessing whether it was worth this much money or not. A few times the auctioneer was close to calling it, when I announced a counter bid.

Three hundred. I closed my eyes, knowing that I'd reached my limit. That was all I had, and as much as I loved this sideboard, I wasn't about to overspend in heat-of-the-moment excitement. The auctioneer paused to once more extol the virtues of this piece of furniture, then continued, asking for three hundred five. Oh, well. At least we'd come home with Henry's entertainment console.

I felt a hand in mine, passing me a folded piece of paper. I looked down to see Henry pull his hand away. The paper I now held wasn't paper. It was a ten-dollar bill. He'd spent thirty of his forty on his purchase, and was slipping me the rest.

"Buy it," he whispered.

I didn't have the heart to tell him that ten dollars most likely wouldn't make a difference at this point. Instead, I shot him a grateful smile and raised my paddle.

"Three ten!"

And then I waited for Metrosexual Man to counter with three fifteen or three twenty and win the sideboard. Imagine my surprise when the auctioneer badgered the man, repeatedly urging him to bid higher. Metrosexual Man pursed his lips and narrowed his eyes, considering the situation. Then he shook his head.

"Going once. Going twice. Sold to the lady for three-ten, bidder number fifty-one."

Neither of us had any money to spend on additional purchases, so Henry and I made our way to the cashier to settle up. I'd tried repeatedly to give him back his ten dollars, but he refused, insisting that he'd get just as much enjoyment out of the sideboard as I would. I doubted that, but the kid did seem to like his antiques, so maybe having this in our dining room was worth ten dollars to him.

Loading the truck was something I hadn't considered when I'd come to the auction. Back in the day, Eli and I had been young and strong, perfectly capable of manhandling whatever we bought into a truck or onto a trailer. After trying to help Henry with the entertainment console, I realized that I didn't quite have the muscle strength that I'd once had, and that a thirteen-year-old boy wasn't strong enough to lift a piece of furniture up to the bed of a pickup truck with only a sixty-year old woman for assistance.

"Need some help?" a deep voice asked. I turned around with a smile to see a man who looked to be mid-to-late sixties. What hair he had was short and more silver than brown, but his arms were muscular under the tattoos. He looked like he spent a good bit of his life either at the gym or doing physically demanding work, and hadn't slacked off in retirement.

"I'd appreciate it," I told him.

He smiled, dark eyes crinkling up in the corners in an appealing fashion. I got the idea that back in the day, this guy had been a flirty heartbreaker. Actually, I got the idea that he probably still was.

"Matt Poffenberger," he said, holding out his hand.

"Kay Carrera." I shook his hand, noting the callouses and firm grip. "Poffenberger? You're a relative of the owners?" This was an estate auction—the Poffenberger estate. It was a recognizable local name, but not as common as Smith or Jones, so it didn't take any psychic skills to assume he was a relative of some sort.

He nodded. "My parents. Mom died ten years ago, and Dad went into assisted living last winter."

I winced. "I'm so sorry. It must be very difficult to be here watching your parents' belongings go under the gavel."

"It's just stuff. I've got the family photo albums and a few sentimental things, but the rest isn't important," he told me, but there was something about his eyes that made me think this auction was far more difficult than he'd imagined it would be.

He walked over and picked up one end of the entertainment console as if it weighed nothing. Henry picked up the other side, trying for the same casual strength and not quite pulling it off.

"I'll hold the weight if you can get your end up on the truck lift gate," Matt told him.

Henry struggled, but managed to finally eased two legs of the console on the truck bed. The whole time Matt patiently waited, not expressing the slightest bit of frustration even though he had a piece of heavy furniture in his arms.

"Hop on up there and guide it in," Matt instructed. Henry

jumped into the truck bed like a monkey and carefully maneuvered the console in place as if it were a priceless museum artifact.

"Miss Kay's got that sideboard that needs to go in too," Henry told the man, shifting the console to the side to make way for the other piece.

Matt tied the console down, then turned to my sideboard, running a hand over the surface. "This was my mother's favorite piece," he said, his voice full of fond nostalgia.

I didn't ask why he hadn't kept it. My parents both had passed away a long time ago. I knew that as hard as it was to part with things that reminded me of them and my childhood, I couldn't exactly stuff my house full of extra furniture and knickknacks, as Mr. Peter across the street had done. Besides, I might love something from my childhood, but that didn't mean I wanted it gracing my own home. My parents had been all about mid-century Early-American style, but I'd shoot myself before putting a blocky oak-framed sofa with velveteen log cabin print upholstery in the living room.

"I'll take good care of it," I assured him instead. "It's beautiful. I was lucky to get it. It will fit right in with all the other nineteenth-century pieces in my house."

He smiled. "Good. I'm pretty sure Mom would haunt me if it didn't go to a good home."

Matt and Henry picked up the sideboard, gently sliding it in next to the entertainment console. Then Matt went off and came back with a few mover's blankets to keep my new acquisition from getting dinged or dirty on the way home.

"Where should I return those?" I asked, not really wanting to come all the way back out here tonight, but feeling a bit guilty about driving off with the blankets.

He waved a hand. "Don't worry about it."

I tucked the edge of a blanket around the corner of the sideboard, securing it under one of the ropes. "I do worry about it. I didn't pay for those, and I doubt they're just laying around for anyone to use. Do you live in Locust Point? Milford? I can swing by and drop them by your house, or we can meet up somewhere."

A look of surprise came over his face, followed by a slow grin that made me realize he'd completely misconstrued my offer as an excuse to see him socially.

"Or I can bring them back here tonight," I added hastily. As much as I didn't want to drive back, it would be better than this man thinking I was asking him on a date.

"Here." He pulled a business card out of his pocket and scribbled a number on the back before handing it to me. "Give me a call and we'll grab a cup of coffee. And you can return the blankets then."

I was sure my face was as red as a tomato in August. "It will be no trouble to bring them back here—"

"After standing in the sun all day at the auction? Go home, relax, and enjoy your new purchase. You can return the blankets later in the week."

Before I could protest further, he'd turned around and headed back to the auction, leaving me staring after him, a business card in my hand.

"I think he likes you," Henry commented.

Great, even a thirteen-year-old boy caught the vibes. How the heck was I going to get out of this one? I envisioned myself downing a cup of coffee in record time, throwing the blankets at Matt Poffenberger, then running out the door of the coffee shop.

"I'm still grieving the loss of my husband," I reminded the boy.

He shrugged, suddenly looking far older than thirteen. "Doesn't mean you can't have a cup of coffee with him. And for the record, I'm totally shipping you guys."

"Shipping us where?" Was this some new slang? What did

mailing packages have to do with a man mistakenly thinking I'd asked him out?

Henry rolled his eyes. "No offense, Miss Kay, but you're old. Come on. I want to get home and show Dad what I bought."

Our new treasures safely tied in the bed of my neighbor's truck, we headed home, Henry singing along to the radio while I smiled in contentment. Awkwardness with Matt Poffenberger aside, it had been an amazing day. Judge Beck had been able to spend some one-on-one time with his daughter Madison, and I'd been able to share something fun with Henry—something he obviously loved. I didn't think Henry had any inclination toward being an auctioneer, but this clearly would be a favorite hobby of his. I knew his father's dream was for Henry to follow in his footsteps as a lawyer, but even lawyers needed an interest outside of work.

As we pulled up to the house, a frown began to crease Henry's forehead. "I don't know, Miss Kay. What am I going to do with this entertainment console? I bought it because it was cool, but maybe I should have just bought a pie safe or something."

I loved that he knew what a pie safe was. "Well, when we get home we'll look on Pinterest and see what other people have done with old entertainment consoles. Maybe that will give you some ideas. In the meantime, you'll want to clean it out, strip down the finish, and see if there's any water damage. If the wood's damaged, you could paint it, or do a faux distressed finish. If the wood's in good shape, then you can think about whether you want to stain it or not."

He bit his lip in thought. "Do you think it could still be a stereo? I mean, I could probably put some Bluetooth speakers in where the old speakers were."

"Sure, that's a cool idea. Audio equipment used to take up a lot more room than it does now, so you'll have a whole lot of space to do something else with." I was envisioning wicker baskets, or drawers.

We pulled into the driveway and went into the house to scare up some assistance in unloading our purchases. Judge Beck and Madison filed out of the house, surveying the contents of the pickup truck bed.

"Dork." Madison elbowed her brother. "What are you going to do with that, play a bunch of old vinyl or something?"

I began to rush to Henry's defense, only to bite my tongue. The boy didn't seem distressed by his sister's teasing. He looked at the console and tilted his head.

"Yeah. I'll do Bluetooth speakers and a turntable, so I can connect my phone, or play old vinyl. That would be cool."

"See? There you go," I told him, lowering the tailgate and scrambling up into the bed to ease my new treasure out of the truck.

"That's really pretty, Miss Kay," Madison proclaimed as she took one side of the sideboard while her father took the other. Judge Beck had the look on his face of a man who had hauled many heavy purchases into his home through the years. Resigned, without opinion.

"Dining room?" the judge asked, quirking an eyebrow.

"Yep." I'd cleared a spot in anticipation, even though I knew how horrible I'd feel coming home empty-handed and seeing that blank wall on the other side of the dining room table.

"Where does Henry's monstrosity go?" Madison asked, climbing the stairs backward. "On the curb for Wednesday's garbage collection?"

This time Henry's face was momentarily crestfallen before he quickly recovered and stuck out his tongue at his sister.

"That's enough, Madison." Judge Beck's voice was sharp.

"This is a new hobby for Henry. Don't be cruel."

Her face fell, and for a second I thought I saw tears in her eyes. "I'm sorry. I was just teasing."

I'd been an only child, but I knew how siblings could annoy each other to the point where anyone else would consider it bullying. And I knew that those very same siblings would beat the snot out of anyone who so much as looked wrong at their brother or sister. It was a bond I'd always wished I'd had growing up, one I'd hoped that my own children would have.

Funny how life often has different plans for us.

"Henry's 'monstrosity'," I said, playing the peacemaker as always, "will go out back under the gazebo where it will be refinished and turned into a thing of incredible beauty. Like a butterfly emerging from a chrysalis."

Madison snorted, casting quick glance at her father.

Henry smiled. "It's going to be awesome. Just you see. I'll work really hard, then if I decide not to keep it, I'll sell it on Craigslist for double the money."

I didn't have the heart to tell him that "double the money" would equate to about fifty cents per hour. Refinishing furniture was often a labor of love.

Madison and the judge wedged their way through the narrow doors of my old Victorian house, shuffling their way into the dining room where they placed my new sideboard with appropriate reverence in its place of glory.

Then we all stood back for a moment of silence as we beheld its beauty.

"I thought Miss Kay wasn't going to win it," Henry whispered loudly to his father. "It was getting expensive."

The judge nodded. "I'm glad she won. It is pretty, and it looks perfect with the mahogany table."

It did. I beamed with satisfaction, and followed the crew out to remove Henry's purchase from the truck. His didn't garner the same admiration, but I had no doubt that after the boy had applied himself, it would be amazing. Or not. Either way, it was thirty bucks. That was a small price to pay for exploring what could be a new hobby. If he lost interest and gave up, I might refinish it myself, or discreetly send it off to the dump. But I had a feeling that Henry had the same kind of stubborn determination that drove his father to burn the candle late into the night, studying briefs and reviewing cases. He'd stick with it. And if he hated it, then this would be his last project. But if he loved it, we'd be able to spend lots of enjoyable weekends at auctions and yard sales in the coming years.

Years. Because he was thirteen, and I hoped that even after the judge and his kids moved out and had their own place, we'd still be friends. I hoped that when I was ancient and he was grown with a family of his own, we'd still be friends. All of them. Friends, and maybe even close enough to be considered adopted-family.

With the entertainment console snug under the gazebo, protected by a tarp from the rain, we went inside and scrounged the leftovers for dinner. The kids headed upstairs for the night, and Judge Beck retreated to the dining room table that often served as his after-hours work desk. I snuck downstairs with my knitting and a pot of hot tea to watch some old mystery movie. Just as the bad guy was about to strike and the music ramped up the tension, Taco hopped on the back of the sofa, purring in my ear and rubbing his face against my hair. I nearly jumped a foot in the air. Then I laughed and gathered my cat on my lap where he snuggled close. I stroked his soft fur, that familiar shadow that I'd come to think of as the ghost of my late husband, Eli, hovering at the end of the couch.

"I think it's the butler," I told the ghost, even though I'd read the book and knew full well it wasn't the butler. If Eli had been here, he would have scoffed at my weak deductive skills and listed all of the facts that supported his theory of who the murderer was. And at the end, he was usually just as wrong as I was. We'd laugh, thankful that neither of us were detectives by profession, then surf the channels to see what else we could watch.

The shadow was silent, not acknowledging my comment. That seemed to make the ache of loss even worse, bringing the sting of tears to my eyes. I clutched Taco to my face, feeling his soft fur and the rumble of his purr, and taking solace that I wasn't alone. I had my cat. I had a family upstairs that I was growing to love. I had friends that I cared about, that cared about me.

But I didn't have Eli.

It was near midnight when I headed upstairs. Judge Beck was no longer in the dining room, his files and papers once more neatly boxed and stacked to the side where he could easily grab them on his way to work on Monday morning. I stood in the dim light reflected from the hallway, holding my cat, admiring my new purchase. The wood inlay was stunning, the finish perfect. Someone had loved this piece of furniture. Someone had taken great care of it for the last twelve decades, because it was pristine, and few pieces survived that long without dents and dings, rings from condensation, or burns from cigarettes.

My sense of warm satisfaction was abruptly shattered with a bitter chill that made my flesh rise. Taco yowled and jumped from my arms, scurrying into the other room with his tail fluffed out. A darkness from the corner of the room coalesced, forming into a bipedal shape near the sideboard. This wasn't the shadow I'd come to associate with Eli; this one was different. I was sure it was a woman. And as she reached out a limb to stroke the top of the sideboard, I felt an incredible sadness…and an aching sense of guilt.

CHAPTER 2

"My new sideboard is haunted," I told Daisy as the early morning sun shone down on our Child's Pose. "I was hoping Eli would chase the new ghost away, but he doesn't seem bothered by her presence."

Anyone listening to me would think I was ready for the looney bin. Luckily, Daisy was one of the only people who'd not attributed my experiences as either a visual impairment from my cataract surgery, or a psychological reaction of grief from the loss of my husband.

"Huh. Well, didn't you get it from some estate sale auction? Maybe the former owners were particularly attached to it. You should bring a psychic in to read the energy."

If I'd lived alone, or Eli had still been alive, I might have done so. Eli would have thought the whole thing to be great fun. We would have had friends over, and all gathered around to hear the psychic's pronouncements about the haunted sideboard. Then we would have had martinis and canapes and possibly a rousing game of bridge, following. I doubted Judge Beck would be as amused by a psychic reading of my new piece of furniture.

Daisy's comment did give me an idea, though. "It was from the estate of Maurice and Eleonore Poffenberger. I met the son at the auction, and he did say his mother really loved this sideboard."

"Well, there you go," Daisy told me smugly.

There had to a reason beyond sentimental attachment for a ghost to be hanging out around a piece of furniture. "She died ten years ago, according to him. The husband, Matt's father, is still alive and in assisted living. Why would she be haunting it for this long a time? Unless you think she suddenly just started appearing because she's not happy her son sold her favorite antique?"

"*Matt?*" Trust Daisy to zoom in on that. "How old is this son? Is he handsome? When you said you met him at the estate auction, I didn't realize that involved enough conversation to be on a first-name basis with him."

"It's the twenty-first century, Daisy. Everyone is on a first-name basis with everyone." Well, aside from my inability to address Judge Beck by his first name, that is. "He looks like he's a few years older than me. And he helped Henry and I load our purchases into the truck. We didn't exactly have what I'd call a lengthy conversation."

Then I thought of the business card I'd crammed into my purse, and that I was supposed to go have coffee with this man in order to return the moving blankets, and nearly toppled out of my Vrikshasana pose.

"Okay, okay. Don't get your panties in a knot, just asking." Daisy grinned at me and winked. "About your new ghost: I don't think she'd suddenly appear when the sideboard was sold, unless maybe if you were chopping it up for kindling or something. And it's unlikely she's been haunting it for ten years just because she's fond of it. Ghosts attached to sentimental objects tend to fade after a few years. If she's still here, it's for another reason, and the sideboard is just the anchor."

If she was here for a reason, maybe she'd leave once I found out what that reason was. All the other ghosts, excepting Eli, that is, had shown up because they were murdered. I hadn't gotten the idea that there had been any foul play in Matt's mother's death, but that wasn't exactly the thing I'd expect someone to reveal to a complete stranger. "I guess I could do some research on the mother to see if she died mysteriously."

"Not all ghosts you see are necessarily murder victims," Daisy cautioned. "Eli's ghost isn't. He's probably still here out of attachment to you and what he feels might be unfinished business, although a psychic could tell you more. Just because the other ghosts were murdered, doesn't mean this one was. Maybe she was estranged from a friend, and never made her peace with him or her. Maybe she and her husband had a fight, and she just can't leave until she tells him she loves him one more time. Or maybe she's staying around for him like Eli is for you, and her ghost just got transferred to your house instead of the assisted living place because she'd firmly attached her spirit to the sideboard."

I chuckled, thinking for a few moments about what material belongings I might link to after death to remain in this plane of existence. If I got hit by a bus this afternoon, I might want to stick around to make sure Taco was taken care of, and maybe float around to see Madison and Henry's graduation, but that was about it.

It all made me think that I probably should be revisiting my will. Not that I had any intention of getting hit by a bus, but with Eli gone and no immediate family, I'd need to make my wishes clear in a legal manner, or risk my estate being tied up in probate for who knows how long.

"Is Pierson going to put a raft in the regatta this year?"

I blinked at the change of topic. Our former mayor had always pestered J.T. until he'd given in and entered a raft. Now that he was in jail, I wasn't sure J.T. would bother. And that would be a shame. The regatta was a big town event, the entrance fees went to support the local food bank, and it was a significant public relations and marketing move to put a raft in the race. People took note of the sponsoring companies, and those were the ones that got the business as being a true part of our community.

Besides that, the regatta was a blast. Everyone lined up along the river with picnics and made a day of it, watching the various races, and laughing as some of the less-seaworthy rafts sank, dunking their crew in the murky waters.

"He hasn't mentioned it. I'm not sure if he'll have time to pull it together by next month."

"Just as well. You know he'd try to rope you into crewing the thing. And probably me, too." Daisy grimaced. "What's up with him lately, anyway? The last reality-show video of his that I was in he kept dropping hints about me inviting him to dinner."

That was totally my fault. I'd jokingly told J.T. to expect knife rests and a high level of etiquette the next time he had dinner at Daisy's, and he'd taken me seriously. I think my boss had a thing for my best friend, but from the I-just-ate-a-lemon look on her face, it clearly wasn't reciprocated.

"Are you in his next video? I think he's doing one about that shoplifting case this week." Thankfully *I* wasn't going to be in this video. As amusing as J.T.'s YouTube channel productions of Gator Pierson, Private Eye were, they interfered with my ability to get my actual job done. Each time I had a cameo, I ended up having to take work home with me that night—and my boss was far too cheap to pay me overtime for that work.

"No. I've been in five so far. I think it's time to take a break from my unpaid amateur acting career and before I go crazy and end up needing your bail bond services myself."

After yoga, and our usual coffee-and-muffins, Daisy headed out and I got ready to go in to the office for a little Sunday catch-up work. We'd been busy lately, and I hated the thought of coming in Monday morning to a whole stack of overdue work. Mondays were enough of a shock to the system without sweating through impossible deadlines.

Mondays were also tough because I'd spent the last ten years of my life taking care of Eli and not heading to a nine-to-five. Helping a physically and cognitively disabled husband was a twenty-four-seven job, but it was one I could do without wearing business casual. Heck, most days I even did it without showering, I'm embarrassed to admit.

I showered and changed, then came down to find chaos in my kitchen and dining room. The kids were leaving today for a week with their mother, and they were clearly running late. Madison and Henry were dashing around with Pop Tarts shoved in their mouths, trying to find laptops and essential items that had migrated throughout the house over the last week all while Judge Beck loaded his golf clubs in the car and poured the rest of the coffee in his travel mug.

"Spending Sunday on the golf course?" I asked, grabbing my own mug of coffee.

"I figured I'd get in eighteen holes after I dropped the kids off at Heather's." He hesitated. "Did you need me home at a certain time?"

He was my roommate, not my spouse, and thus free to come and go as he pleased without any need to notify me about his whereabouts, but I did appreciate the courtesy in his question.

"No, I'm going to try to get some work done today in the

office. Get ahead of schedule. I'll just grab some takeout for dinner."

"Good grief, even I don't work on Sundays," he teased. "Don't make a habit of this, Kay." Then he turned and yelled for Madison and Henry, letting them know that they needed to leave *right now*.

The kids surprised me with quick hugs before their father shooed them out the door, telling me they'd see me next week. It brought tears to my eyes. I'd gotten used to having them here, and each time it was Heather's turn for custody, I felt a horrible ache in my chest. I can only imagine how tough this was on Judge Beck, or even on Heather when it wasn't her week with the kids.

I waved them off as they headed down the street, then climbed into my own car, making my way through unusually busy traffic to the office. Milford was the larger city, only five miles away from Locust Point, but our smaller town was actually the county seat and home to both the courthouse and the sheriff's office. The old courthouse had been smack in the middle of downtown, but a fire in the early part of the last century had given the town council the opportunity to move it to the outskirts where they could expand parking, and where there was plenty of room for law offices and bail bond companies. Pierson Investigative & Recovery Services was only a few blocks away from the police station, and a few miles from the courthouse. I'd always thought J.T. would be better served having offices closer to the courthouse where so many of his bail bond clients were arraigned, but he found it made better sense to be close to the police officers who sent him plenty of leads. Over the years, that side of the business had shrank, as had the old gumshoe private investigative work, and J.T. found himself with more clients that needed to track down debtors to recover assets. Even the divorce clients' needs had changed. Instead of prowling around on cheating spouses with a camera in hand, they wanted forensic accountants to find hidden checking accounts, or internet research specialists to find proof of cheating, or drug use through online sites.

That's where I came in. I'd been a journalism major, and until Eli's accident, I'd made my living by being a reporter for major publications as well as researching and writing freelance feature pieces for magazines and newspapers. After the accident, I'd juggled taking care of Eli with the odd freelance work, but it had become clear over the years that journalism had changed.

All those research skills made me ideally suited to perform the skip tracing and online investigative work that J.T. needed. He did the occasional gumshoe work, ran the business, interfaced with the clients and schmoozed with the police and various paralegals and courthouse employees to get leads and information, while I typed at a computer and kept the clients whose business paid the majority of the bills happy. It was a good partnership, and as quirky as my boss was with his YouTube reality show obsession, I liked him.

I flicked on the lights and fired up the coffee maker, then eyed the stack of folders on my desk. I grabbed a cup and reviewed what I needed to handle right away versus what could wait for later in the week. There was a stack of skip traces for our biggest client, Creditcorp, then two bail bond applicants to review for risk, and some digging around for a divorce client.

The bail bond ones were a priority since we needed to get those squared away and get the clients out of jail as soon as possible. I finished those by noon, wrapped up two of the easier Creditcorp files, then spent some time on the very distasteful divorce case. I always hated this part of the work. It was one thing to see the poor decisions and behavior of potential bail clients and those who were delinquent on accounts, but there was so much emotion in these divorce cases. The woman I was checking out for J.T. this time had taken out half a dozen credit cards where it seemed she'd forged her husband's signature. She'd also posted Facebook photos on a secondary account showing her trip to Bermuda with a much younger man, all while her primary account said she was home with her kids, taking them to the park and the arcade.

I wrote up my summary and looked at the clock, debating which file to go through next. They would all take far longer than the three hours I had left before I'd planned on leaving, and I was feeling deflated and tired from the work on the divorce case. I needed a quick break before digging into the other Creditcorp files, and what better break than taking an hour and researching the woman who had previously owned my sideboard—and who was most likely the one haunting it.

CHAPTER 3

I quickly discovered that Maurice and Eleonore Poffenberger hadn't lived a very newsworthy life. Nor had the pair been at all active on social media. I dug through courthouse records and both birth and death announcements and found that Maurice was born in 1928 in Milford and had been a surveyor for a local contractor until his retirement. Eleonore had been born in 1926 and had, as her son had said, passed away ten years ago. Her obituary listed her as a housewife and mother, survived by both her husband and their son, Matthew Poffenberger. Her maiden name had been Hansen, and her parents, both long dead, had been Harlen and Mabel. Hansen was a recognizable local name. Harlen had owned the downtown department store where pretty much everyone had shopped in Locust Point from 1910 until his death in 1945. Curious, I dug back through the newspaper archives until I found a picture of the man, chuckling a bit at his round pot belly proudly accented by the chain of a pocket watch, and his shrewd eyes behind wire-rimmed glasses. He had a big bushy mustache which made me wonder how he managed to keep it out of his food while eating.

Hansen's had been a heck of a department store. Not that I'd been alive when it had been open, but I remembered my mom and grandmother talking about it. It had been three stories of quality clothing and accessories, with a system of vacuum-sent containers to transport invoices and pricing information from the upper floors down to the cashiers. From what my mother had said, it was a lot like some banks still use, and it had fascinated her as a child. She'd kept one of the coats my grandmother had bought her from there, and shown it to me—dusky blue wool with a navy silk lining, and the Hansen's tag inside the collar.

None of this had anything to do with my sideboard or the ghost I was assuming was Eleonore Poffenberger, but I was too far down the rabbit hole to stop now, so I dug around further, curious about this Mabel who'd snagged the town's most eligible bachelor from the early part of the last century.

Harlen had been born in 1872, and from the town records, hadn't married Mabel until 1926, the same year their daughter and only child had been born. Fifty-four seemed a bit old to be tying the knot for the first time. I'd imagined by then the guy would have been pretty entrenched in bachelorhood and reluctant to marry, but once I found a picture of Mabel, I understood his sudden change of heart. She'd been nineteen at the time of their marriage, and by the picture in the newspaper, the woman had been a stunning beauty.

Mabel had the iconic 1920's short bob of dark hair that curled at the ends around the cheekbones of her heart-shaped face. Her eyes were doe-like, her mouth the perfect cupid's bow. Her figure was made for the drop-waist, straight and loose dresses and she looked positively adorable in a cloche hat with a curved brim.

Just as the paper had been filled with mentions of Harlen Hansen and his store, his social activities, and his charitable donations, there were just as many mentions of Mabel Stevens and her sister Lucille. Both were quite in demand at parties and society events, and their names seemed to be mentioned everywhere. They were twins, and from the old pictures I could find, they were nearly indistinguishable from each other.

Of course, none of this was helping me with my ghost identification. One specter in my house was enough. I'd come to enjoy the ghost I associated with Eli, but didn't particularly want a second one hanging around.

I'd needed to call Matt Poffenberger to return the moving blankets. If we were going to have a cup of coffee together, then it would be the perfect time to ask him some questions about his mother. It might be a bit rude to ask him point blank how she'd passed away, but maybe if I got him talking about her and her life, I could find out why she was haunting my sideboard. Of course, there was no guarantee that my figuring out if she was murdered and if so, who was responsible, would result in the ghost heading toward the light and leaving my house and furniture alone, but it was worth a try. If it didn't work, and Eleonore proved to be too much of a pain, I guess I could always sell the sideboard.

But I didn't want to do that. I already loved that piece of furniture and hated the thought of having to part with it. Honestly, I could understand how Eleonore could haunt the sideboard. I'd had it for less than twenty-four hours and I was already becoming attached to it.

Calling it a day, I packed a box full of files that would have rivaled the ones Judge Beck had been spreading across my dining room table, and made my way home. It was June, and the kids had been out of school for a few weeks. I'd gotten used to them being there, lounging on the sofa with their headphones and laptops, or out in the hot tub, or playing video games. It felt weird to come home to a silent house—well, silent except for a very upset cat.

Taco wasn't happy about being cooped up in the house, but at least with the kids here he got slipped snacks and was showered with affection. He'd nearly snuck out the door on my way to the office this morning, and I was half expecting to find that he'd knocked over a lamp or shredded some upholstery. Luckily, he hadn't done either, and his mood improved considerably once I poured some Happy Cat into his food bowl.

I'd made dinner, eaten it, put the leftovers away, and was halfway through knitting a baby cap to add to the growing stack of hats I was planning to take to the hospital this month when Judge Beck finally came through the door. He was energetic and cheerful, lugging his bag of golf clubs behind him.

"Ready for the PGA?" I asked, pausing in my knitting.

He laughed. "I'm the next Jack Nicklaus. By the way, there's a storm moving in," he warned me. "Might want to roll the windows up in your car."

I jumped to my feet, wishing for the days when we actually did roll the windows up and I didn't need a car key to do so. "I cooked instead of getting take-out. There's leftover pork chops in the fridge along with a salad I made. Help yourself," I told him, digging in my purse for my keys.

The judge vanished into the dining room and I dashed out the door, eyeing the sky with alarm. How had those dark clouds moved in without my noticing? It was close to dusk. It would have been hard to tell without a clock as the line of dark to the west completely blocked out the sun. I ran to the car and put up my windows, feeling the first few huge drops as I finished.

I was going to get completely soaked, but I needed to make sure the tarp was secure over Henry's entertainment console before the wind and rain picked up. Lightning flashed as I ran, the thunder directly afterward. I adjusted the tarp on the console, securing it tighter as the wind began to rush through the trees. Within seconds, the sky had opened up and I stood, watching the streaks of lightning and shivering as the cold rain blew sideways into the gazebo.

Lights came on in the house. The back door opened. Just as I was about to make a run for it, I saw a figure emerge, carrying a giant golf umbrella. Judge Beck to the rescue.

He was wet from the sideways rain by the time he joined me in the gazebo.

"Taxi service?" I teased as he extended the umbrella over my head.

"I'm afraid my knight in shining armor impulse was better in idea than it was in action," he confessed. "You're probably going to be just as wet as you would have been without the umbrella."

"I still appreciate it," I told him. "Are you ready to run for it?"

"One. Two. Three." We both ran, the judge wrapping an arm around my shoulder to hold me close enough to get the maximum benefit of the umbrella. It didn't matter. Ten feet from the stairs, a huge gust of wind came up, turning the umbrella inside out and drenching both of us with icy rain. I squealed, abandoning my knight in a mad dash for the door.

He was right behind me, and we both stood dripping puddles of water onto the kitchen floor, laughing. The judge waved his destroyed umbrella, spraying additional water around the room and causing me to laugh even harder. Then I caught sight of the plate on the counter with the warmed-up pork chop and salad, as well as the glass of iced tea. He'd been reheating his dinner and seen me out in the gazebo, then come to my rescue. It was so sweet, and something no one besides my father or Eli would have done for me.

"Go change out of your wet clothes," he told me. "I'll clean up here."

He truly was a knight in shining armor. I thanked him and raced up the stairs. And by the time I came back down wearing my fuzzy pajamas and slippers, I had an idea. Judge Beck's birthday was next week. Both kids had carefully wrapped presents upstairs for their father, and Madison was planning on cooking an elaborate dinner as well as a special cake with my help, but I wanted to do something in addition to that.

I'd been thinking about having a neighborhood barbeque for a while now and it was far past time I put those plans into action. I was long overdue on introducing him to the neighborhood. We could make it adults-only, hold it this coming weekend before the kids returned from Heather's, and if anyone overindulged, they could easily stagger home. It would be my sort-of birthday gift to the man who'd really become like family to me.

"What are you doing this weekend?" I asked as I walked into the dining room. Judge Beck had changed into his own pair of pajama pants and t-shirt, and was, as usual, at the table with papers spread out in front of him. This time, though, a ghostly shadow stood just a few feet to the side of him near the edge of the sideboard. It was weird seeing her there. It was even weirder that Judge Beck was completely oblivious to her presence.

"This weekend? Uh…."

I realized by the expression on his face that I'd made another faux pas just like the one I'd made with Matt Poffenberger. The judge's brain had clearly gone into "she's-asking-me-on-a date mode".

"No. I mean, not like that. I'm planning a neighborhood get together, and wanted to make sure you'd be there to meet everyone. Plus, your birthday is next week, so I thought it would be fun to do a barbeque-and-meet-the-neighbors thing."

"Oh." He smiled. "That sounds great. I'm playing golf Saturday, but our tee time is early, so any time after two should be okay. Or Sunday, although the kids are coming over around five."

"Saturday then. I'll arrange it for the evening, like around six?"

"That would be good. Thanks."

He returned to his work and I went back to the other room, putting aside my knitting and pulling out my laptop and my Creditcorp files. After a few hours, I gave up and retreated back to the sofa and my knitting once more. It seemed weird for us to be in two different rooms, just one wall away, but I didn't want to interrupt his work. And having a ghost standing in the corner of the room would have been a bit disconcerting, so I stayed in the parlor, acutely aware of the creak of the dining room chair, and the noise of papers being moved around. Around midnight, I heard the judge packing up his files, and setting the box by the door. He paused by the parlor, looking in at me, but by the time I'd reached the end of the row and looked up, he'd gone—up to bed presumably.

But no. A minute later he returned, carrying a book. "Mind if I join you?"

"Not at all," I told him.

So, there we sat, the only sound the ticking of my grandfather clock and Taco's purring. I knitted. He read his book. And around one in the morning, we both rose and headed up the stairs—the judge to his room and I to mine. The rain started up again, drumming on the roof and tapping on the

CHAPTER 4

*T*here were additional files on my desk when I got in Monday morning along with a note from J.T. saying he was at the courthouse and would be back in the afternoon. I dug right in, clearing out three cases, then I pulled Matt Poffenberger's business card out of my purse.

The number on the back was written in a sharp, bold hand. I stared at it a minute, then flipped it over, wondering where the man worked.

It turned out that Matthew Poffenberger was a retired Master Sergeant with the US. Air Force and was on the board of directors for a non-profit called Stand Strong.

I was stalling, so I Googled the organization, which funded a hotline and a variety of suicide prevention programs aimed at veterans as well as first responders. Matt was indeed on the board of directors, and ran local therapy groups as well. Curious, I did a search on Matt and found that he was active at the local VFW and ran several fundraisers for the volunteer fire department, and an at-risk youth program in Milford. It seemed that Matt had inherited his grandfather's community action bent, although I got the idea Harlen had done it more as a form of PR for his business, where Matt was doing all of this fairly under the radar. He wasn't in the paper beyond a tiny mention every year or so, and it took some digging to uncover all his charitable work.

Unable to put it off any longer, I dialed the number on the back of the card and nearly hung up when the man answered, barking out his name like he was going to follow it up with a command for me to drop and give him twenty.

"Hi, Matt. It's Kay Carrera from the auction? You helped me load the sideboard and entertainment console into my truck? And loaned me some moving blankets? I wanted to see if you were free in the next few days so I could return them."

"Kay!" His voice changed, becoming softer and warmer. "I was hoping you'd call, and not just because of the moving blankets. Are you free for lunch today?"

I suddenly felt like I wanted to run and hide under a bush, like a spooked rabbit. He had misunderstood me at the auction, and now I had to figure out how to let him know I wasn't interested without hurting his feelings.

"I really can't do lunch, but maybe a cup of coffee?" Coffee was not like a date, right?

"When? I'm down at the VFW right now helping get set up for bingo night tonight. Do you want to just swing by?"

Now that didn't sound at all like a date. I sighed in relief. "Perfect. How about eleven?"

"It's a date," he said, sending me back into panic-land. "See you then."

I stared at my cell phone for a moment, wondering how I should proceed. He'd helped me load my furniture, loaned me blankets. He seemed like a really nice guy, a good person, someone that I wouldn't have minded meeting for lunch or even dinner had my situation been different. But as nice and attractive as Matt Poffenberger was, nothing stirred in my heart when I thought of him. Actually, the thought of dating any man made me feel numb inside. I'd loved Eli. We'd built an amazing life together. After his accident when he hadn't been the same, I'd still loved him and built a life with him—a different one, but one I still missed deeply. I didn't have it in me to love another that way. My well was dry when it came to that particular kind of love, and I wasn't sure it would ever be refilled again.

But I was being silly. This was just a cup of coffee in a VFW hall with a kind man who'd helped me out. I'd ask him about his mother and the sideboard, give him back his blankets, and if he asked me out, I'd very nicely tell him that I was a recent widow and not ready for dating.

I wasn't sure I ever *would* be ready for dating. And that was fine with me. Some people go through their whole lives without finding a love like Eli and I had. We'd been blessed, and I wasn't about to spend my time trying to recreate what we had. My love was for my friends, for Daisy and Madison and Henry and Taco. And Judge Beck, in a friendly roommate kind of way.

But as I got ready to head out to the VFW, I thought of Matt loading the furniture in the truck with Henry, and his charming smile. I wasn't ready for romance, but there was plenty of room in my heart for more friends.

* * *

Matt was unfolding tables and setting them in rows when I arrived with the moving blankets neatly folded in my arms. He looked up, smiled, then turned to the other men and said a few words before walking toward me with a purposeful stride.

I couldn't help but scrutinize him anew, looking for a

resemblance to the pictures I'd seen yesterday of his grandparents. He had a lively expression that was a faint echo of his beautiful grandmother, but beyond that, I couldn't see any strong likeness. He definitely didn't look anything like his grandfather who'd had a potbelly, a mustache, and a perceptive gaze. The perceptive gaze was there, but that could just as easily have come from his military career. No, he was nothing at all like the pictures of Harlen Hansen. Matt was just shy of six feet tall, clean shaven and built like a man who had spent his prime years of life hitting the gym hard. I guess he must have resembled his father's instead of his mother's side of the family.

"I'm glad you called." He smiled and the corners of his dark brown eyes creased in deep lines. "Are you enjoying the sideboard? I'm thrilled that it went to a good home. Like I said, I'm pretty sure that Mom would haunt me if it hadn't."

That was amazingly close to the topic I'd wanted to discuss. "I'm thrilled that I managed to buy it. It's a beautiful piece of furniture, obviously well taken care of and loved. I was actually hoping you could give me more information on it, as well as talk with me about your mother."

He took that in stride, and motioned me over to a table that looked like it was already set up for tonight's bingo activities. "I'm all yours. How do you take your coffee?"

I took a seat, setting the blankets on the table in front of me. The 'all yours' comment knocked me off balance, but I managed to reply that I drank my coffee black, no sugar. Then I watched him head off through a swinging door to the kitchen. The other two guys setting up tables were watching me on the sly, shifting their work closer, no doubt so they could overhear. I heard the squawk of the swinging door and saw Matt returning, two steaming mugs in his hands.

"It's not that horrible," he told me as he handed me a mug. "I made it myself so it's fresh and stronger than the brown water those guys like to make." His voice raised in volume as he mentioned the other men, who shouted back a friendly criticism of Matt's brewing ability, advising me that I'd probably need a spoon to drink my beverage.

"So, the sideboard." Matt took a sip of his coffee and leaned back in his chair, tilting it up on two legs. "I'm not really an antique-head, so I don't know much about what it is or how old it is, but I'm happy to share what I do know. Dad would have more information on how long it had been in Mom's family and the history of it, but it's hit or miss with him nowadays."

I nodded sympathetically, assuming that the elder Mr. Poffenberger most likely suffered from dementia or Alzheimer's.

"You said that the sideboard was one of your mother's favorite pieces?" I asked.

"Let's just say that in a fire, I'm sure she would have dragged that sideboard out before the photo albums. Mom came from a wealthy family, but Dad was from the other side of the tracks, so to speak. The sideboard had been a wedding gift to Mom from her mother, and it was a high-quality piece of furniture. The rest of our stuff was thrift-store or yard-sale. Mom cherished that sideboard. I'm pretty sure it had been Grandma's before, because Mom had mentioned that the sideboard was supposed to go to me, and then on to my daughter at her wedding. I don't have any kids, and as much as I loved my mother, it's not exactly my style of furniture." He laughed. "I'm glad she didn't give it to me as a wedding gift, or one of my exes would have probably taken it in the divorce."

One of his exes? I winced, wondering how many times Matt Poffenberger had been married. Sometimes people grew apart, or changed, or a partner did something unforgivable that shattered their marriage, but a pattern of that indicated poor judgment of character in my opinion. Although it was probably easy for me to be snobby about it since I'd truly had the until-death-do-we-part marriage. I thought of Judge Beck and Heather, about how their divorce seemed to be hurting them both equally. They were good people. I wasn't sure what exactly had gone wrong in their marriage, but the end of it seemed so tragic. Maybe I shouldn't be so quick to judge.

"Honestly, Mom's probably happier that you have the sideboard than me," he confessed. "I would have dented it, or left a wet glass on it and marred the finish, or something."

Yikes. It seemed from what he said that it was just a favorite piece of furniture, and that Eleonore was sticking around to make sure I didn't chop it up for firewood or paint it fluorescent pink or something. Hopefully she'd be reassured and vanish in the next day or two, but remembering the conversation with Daisy, I thought I should check further.

"How did your mom die?"

His face fell. "Cancer. She fought it for five years. I'm not sure my dad will ever get over it. She was a strong woman, cheerful and positive until the very end, but it was tough to watch her go through all those treatments and surgeries."

My heart ached, and I couldn't help but reach out and put my hand on top of his. "It's hard when you lose someone you've loved for so long."

He looked down at my hand and nodded. "She used to say that she wished she'd gone quick, like her mother had. Grandma had a stroke. No suffering, no treatments, no surgeries. She was completely fine, fixing sandwiches for lunch, then down she went. Mom said she'd complained her right hand felt funny just before the stroke, but she had arthritis, and didn't think anything of it."

I clenched my jaw for a moment to hold back tears.

"That's how my husband died. He'd been in an accident ten years prior, and had limited use of his legs and arms as well as a brain injury that affected his speech and thought process. I always wondered if I'd called the ambulance too late. Looking back, I think maybe he was having symptoms of the stroke all day, but I missed the signs."

Matt turned his hand over, gripping mine in his. "I'm so sorry, Kay. When did your husband die?"

I steadied my breathing. "Four months ago."

He stilled. I looked up and saw the expression in his eyes. "I'm so sorry. I can't claim to know what you're going through, but I saw how my father grieved. Losing someone you've loved for so long is probably the most difficult thing in life."

I sniffed and pulled my hand away with a wobbly smile. This isn't how I wanted our coffee-not-a-date to go. Yes, Matt probably now realized that I wasn't romantically interested, but I hadn't meant to convey that by baring my soul and nearly crying.

"Anyway," he continued softly. "I'm sure that Mom is thrilled someone has the sideboard that truly appreciates it. And now you can pass it down to your children."

I almost blurted out that I didn't have children, but I'd revealed enough acutely personal information to this man I'd just met. Besides, his words immediately conjured up an image of Madison and Henry. I wasn't sure Madison would be interested, but Henry would certainly love inheriting the sideboard. Besides, it was his ten dollars that allowed me to have the winning bid.

"I read that your mom was Harlen Hansen's daughter," I said, trying to ease the conversation into a less emotion-heavy direction.

Matt grinned, leaning back in his chair once more, again balancing it on the two rear legs. "She was. He died before I was born, and Mom never had a bad word to say about anyone, but from what my father told me, Harlen Hansen was a real jerk."

He'd been married to a nineteen-year-old at the age of fifty-four and suddenly a father. I could understand that he might not be parent of the year.

"He was just...cold. From what Dad said, he had very little to do with Mom or Grandma. He spent long hours in the store, lots of time with his buddies playing cards and drinking scotch, and he liked to golf. Other than sitting absolutely silent at dinner each night, he was hardly in the same room with his wife or daughter. Dad said it seemed like he never even spoke to them, and he thought that maybe Grandma was afraid of him, although no one ever accused him of laying a hand on her." He chuckled. "Probably never laid a hand on her in the bedroom past their wedding night either, given that they only had the one child."

That was shocking—not so much because Matt was indulging in vulgar speculation about his grandparents' sex life, but because I'd seen pictures of Mabel. She'd been gorgeous, vivacious, and evidently on everyone's guest list. "Why had he bothered to marry her?" I asked, indulging in some vulgar speculation of my own. "She was a stunning beauty at nineteen, and he was a fifty-four-year-old bachelor. Why get married at all if he wasn't in love, or at the very least incredibly physically attracted to her?"

Matt shrugged. "Who knows? Sometimes people change once they're married. Maybe he was wildly in love, but once the vows were said, he discovered Grandma wasn't the woman he thought she was. Maybe she was a prude in the bedroom and he got tired of trying to light a fire on an iceberg. Or maybe Harlen was the sort of guy who just wanted a beautiful trophy wife that was coveted by all the other guys in town. Maybe he was gay and she was his beard."

I could see any of those except for the second one. It had been the Roaring Twenties. Women and young people were starting to discover their power in the world, to assert themselves and take a stand. And that sometimes included sexuality. Maybe Mabel was a good girl who guarded her reputation and virginity carefully, but I doubt she would have been the type of woman who was an iceberg.

But who was I to judge? I'd come of age in the early seventies when women were demanding equal rights and the same opportunities as men. I'd been raised by two liberal and passionate parents, and I'd been brought up with their support behind me every step of the way. It had been easy for me to go to college, to protest against my government, to have sex with Eli before marriage, and demand that our physical relationship was satisfying for the both of us. Not that I'd ever had to demand that. Eli had been everything I'd ever wanted in a lover, and in a husband.

"Maybe Harlen really sucked in bed and Mabel cut him off," I conjectured, thinking of how I would have reacted if I'd been in that situation.

Matt blinked in surprise, then burst out laughing. "Good point. And I wouldn't blame her one bit. I just can't imagine my grandmother getting it on, let alone being an enthusiastic partner. She lived with us since I was about ten until her death, and she was a stickler for propriety. That woman never missed a church service, insisted we say a prayer every night before dinner. She was always begging for God to forgive her of her sins. I always got the impression that she'd make a Puritan look like a loose woman, but she was probably different when she was young."

"Did you ever see a picture of her back when she was nineteen, right before she got married?" Matthew shook his head, so I got out my phone and pulled up the picture, and showed it to him.

"Wow. She *was* beautiful, although I never really understood the skinny, adolescent-boy figure that was in fashion back then. The Twiggy fad just about made a monk out of me. I like a woman with curves." He said the last with a sheepish grin.

"She had a twin," I told him, wondering what had happened to Lucille. I hadn't gone too far into my research, assuming that anything outside of Eleonore's direct line wasn't relevant.

"Really? I had no idea. She must have died young because neither Mom nor Grandma ever mentioned her."

It happened. And if her twin's death had been a particularly painful spot in Mabel's heart, I could imagine she wouldn't want to discuss her sister's loss. Or perhaps they'd just grown apart, or had a terrible disagreement. Or maybe Lucille had married someone who hadn't lived up to Harlen Hansen's idea of proper society, and Mabel had been forbidden to see or speak with her sister again. I could imagine *that* would have put a huge wedge in their love life.

Although my imagination was probably concocting stories that had no basis in reality.

"Your father lived alone for quite a while after your mother's death," I said to shift the conversation back into the more recent past.

"Ten years. He'd still be in that house, but his health really declined the last few years. He needs a wheelchair and help with bathing and getting his meals, and he's on oxygen now. I smuggle him in potato chips and cookies, but I refuse to bring him cartons of Marlboro Lights. The sale of the house and the proceeds from the auction should be enough to keep him in comfort for the rest of his life, but I'm don't want to hasten that end, if you know what I mean."

I did. But something about his statement puzzled me. "Your mother was the sole child of Harlen Hansen. She should have inherited a fortune. Did they lose the money—" I stopped abruptly, realizing that I was prying into what was absolutely none of my business. If they lost their fortune in the stock market, or squandered it gambling, or were the victims of an embezzlement, it wasn't my place to ask.

"There was no money. I'm not sure why, but I don't remember Grandma being particularly well off when she was living with us. In fact, I got the impression that Mom and Dad were supporting her. When she passed away, I think Dad was scraping together money for her funeral expenses. Maybe Harlen spent it all before he died, or the department store wasn't doing as well as everyone thought."

There was no mystery to be solved that I could tell, just a woman who'd really loved a family heirloom and had somehow attached her psychic energy and spirit to it after her death. Either she'd eventually vanish, or I'd need to get used to a second ghost in my house.

"Thanks, Matt," I told him, rising from the metal folding chair. "I've really enjoyed the conversation and the coffee. Which was most definitely not too strong," I announced loud enough for the other two guys to hear.

He stood as well. "I'm going to visit my dad tomorrow at Tranquil Meadows Nursing Home. I go over to have lunch with him every Tuesday. If you'd like to come along, I'm sure he'd enjoy the company. And you could ask him more questions about the sideboard and Mom."

I hesitated. It was too weird to think that Matt would believe a visit to his elderly father in the nursing home was a date, so I took the offer as just a kind way of helping me research the history of an antique I'd just acquired, and possibly continuing a budding friendship.

CHAPTER 5

*T*ranquil Meadows Nursing Home was a sprawling one-story building on the outskirts of town. The parking lot was depressingly empty, and I was able to park close to the front, walking past a giant three-tier fountain, and in through the automatic double-wide glass doors. A young blonde woman in scrubs with dancing penguins on a turquoise background smiled at me, handing me the guest sign-in book. I let her know that I was here to have lunch with Maurice Poffenberger and his son Matthew, and the girl's face lit up with a smile.

"Oh, we just love Maurice. He's the sweetest man, and he will be thrilled to have two visitors."

She came around the desk and led me down a hall toward where I assumed the cafeteria was. I noted that in spite of my fears, the nursing home did not smell of antiseptic cleaners or latex. Instead, it smelled like fresh baked cookies and apple cinnamon pie. Now this was the sort of place I hoped I ended up when I was unable to care for myself. It seemed less hospital-like and more like a friendly day-camp.

"He's having a good day today," she confided in me.

"Sometimes he gets really confused and doesn't know where he is and asks for his wife. Lots of days he thinks Darren, the RN that is assigned to him, is his son. But today he's sharp as a tack."

She threw open a set of double doors and the smell of chicken and French fries assailed my senses. Instead of the long tables of my high school, these were small round tables with various residents clustered around them. Many of them were in wheelchairs. A few of them had assistants sitting next to them, helping them cut food or even actually feeding them. It warmed my heart that even those who were unable to get a fork to their mouth were still brought to the dining area to enjoy a meal in a communal environment.

I spotted Matt, and told my blonde escort that I could take it from here. He waved at me as I crossed the dining area, then jumped up to pull out a chair on the other side of an elderly man with a tube of oxygen in his nose, and a plate of fried chicken and green beans in front of him.

"I ordered you the chicken," Matt told me with a smile. "It's actually really good. The ladies here bread it with cracker meal and fry it fresh. And the green beans are cooked in bacon grease."

I remembered the hospital food that I'd eaten for months while Eli had been recuperating from the accident, and the cafeteria staff there had been insanely obsessed with healthy, low fat, low carb, low calorie, bland-as-sand food. Green beans cooked with bacon grease sounded heavenly.

As I sat, Matt scooted the chair under me. I turned and smiled at his father. "Hello, Mr. Poffenberger. I'm Kay Carrera. I bought your wife's sideboard and your son invited me here so I could find out more about it. I hear your wife loved that piece of furniture very much."

One of the assisted living staff came over at that moment, placing plates of chicken, French fries, and green beans in front of Matt and I, then turning to encourage the elder Mr. Poffenberger to eat before heading off. The food smelled heavenly, and I didn't hesitate to dig in.

Maurice blinked down at his chicken a few moments before lifting his slightly confused gaze to me. "Carrera. You said your name was Kay Carrera? Are you related to that surgeon fella?"

It was like I'd been stabbed in the chest. "Eli Carrera. Yes. He was my husband."

"Well, he is a darned good surgeon. Saved Ellie's life that time she had that heart attack. I thought I was going to lose her. Love of my life, that woman. Is she coming to have lunch with us today?"

Matt took a bite of chicken. Although he smiled reassuringly at his father, I could see the grief in his eyes. "Not today, Dad. Not today."

Maurice sighed, picking at his green beans. "Most beautiful woman I'd ever seen. I went to high school with her. We'd moved into town my sophomore year, and I walked into algebra and saw this gorgeous girl with black hair and the most beautiful skin. She was wearing a plaid dress that showed off every bit of her amazing figure. I nearly failed that class because all I could do was stare at her. I was afraid to talk to her until a few years after graduation when I finally worked up the nerve to ask her out."

"And you were twenty-two when you got married?"

He laughed. "I was twenty-two. She was twenty-four. My older woman. I've loved her from the moment I met her."

This was so sweet. I was glad I'd come here to meet Mr. Poffenberger. His stories warmed my heart, and even Matt looked misty-eyed at the way his father talked about his mom.

"And she got the sideboard for a wedding gift? From her parents?"

Maurice frowned, looking momentarily confused. "Is that the inlaid buffet thing in the dining room? Her mom gave that to her. I think her mom's sister had owned it. Or maybe her mother. Either way, it had been something Ellie loved from her childhood and she cried when her mother gave it to her as a wedding gift. I swear if we had ended up homeless and living out of our car, she would have kept that thing. She said it had meant a lot to her mother, and that it meant a lot to her." The man suddenly turned to me and tilted his head. "You're Matt's wife, right? It's only fitting you should have it. Ellie wanted it to go to him and to his children."

Matt and I exchanged an awkward glance. "No, Mr. Poffenberger. I'm not married to your son. But I do love the sideboard and I truly cherish it. I'll love it just as much as your wife did."

He nodded, eating a few of his green beans. "That's good. And you can give it to your children."

Again, I felt that knife stab in my heart, and I thought of Henry, loving the sideboard just as much as I did. I needed to take care of my will. Things like this needed to be settled. We ate in silence for a few moments while I thought of what I should will each of Judge Beck's kids, what Daisy might like to have, and what Judge Beck might like to have.

"I wanted to enlist in World War II," Maurice suddenly announced. "I was only eleven when it started, and I used to sit on the beach with my binoculars, trying to see if I could spy enemy planes or subs off the coast. I'd married by the time of the Korean War and couldn't leave Ellie behind to serve. I was so proud when Matt joined the Air Force. He served in two wars, you know. Two. But of course you know that, as his wife and all."

Awkward.

"Dad, Kay isn't my wife, she's a friend," Matt tried to explain.

His father waved his fork in the air and scowled. "Don't hide your light under a bushel, son. Vietnam. The Gulf War. And then all the work you do with those poor soldiers and police officers that can't get what they seen out of their head. He's a good man, Kay. You picked a good one, marrying my son here."

"I truly appreciate his service." I gave Matt a smile and he returned it. I noticed he seemed a bit red in the face at his father's praise. Or maybe it was his father's continued assertions that I was his wife.

We ate, making small talk for a while about the weather, the local high school sports teams, the upcoming regatta. Evidently Matt had promised to check his father out of the nursing home to attend the regatta this year, and Maurice was very excited to attend an event that he hadn't missed in the last twenty years.

We finished our lunch and I noticed a few of the residents had begun to leave the cafeteria. Matt and Maurice lingered, so I accepted a cup of coffee from one of the servers and stayed as well.

"Never much liked Mabel, you know," Maurice suddenly announced.

I stared at him in surprise, thinking of the stunning woman in the photograph. "Why?"

He frowned. "She was a sad woman. A woman with secrets. She loved Ellie with all her heart, showered her with affection, but there was something about her I just didn't like."

Matt sighed. "Maybe it was all the church-going, Dad. You were never a religious sort of guy."

"Maybe." Maurice shook his head. "I dunno. My Ellie was an angel. She was so happy and cheerful, even though her dad barely said two words to her his whole life. Even though he left all his money to some charity rather than her. She didn't care. But Mabel cared. I think that woman had a whole lot of demons in her soul."

Matt sucked in a sharp breath. "Dad. Maybe it's time for you to go back to your room. Grandma was a kind woman. She was just quiet and seemed to be inside herself a lot of the time. You said it yourself. She loved Mom with all of her heart."

Maurice nodded. "She did. That's the only reason I agreed to let her live with us. Well, that and I could never deny Ellie anything she asked of me. That woman was my life, you know. I loved her from the moment I saw her and from that instant, no other could compare. So beautiful and happy. She was like sunshine every day of my life. Is she coming to lunch? She left this morning and I was hoping she'd be back for lunch."

This hurt my heart. Eleonore had been a happy, loving woman, in spite of a distant father and a mother who, from what I was assuming, was prone to depression. Maurice was proud of his son, and had enjoyed a wonderful life. I hoped he continued to imagine that his wife had just gone out this morning and would be back at any moment, because the reality that she'd been dead for ten years might be too much for him to bear.

The reality that my husband had been dead for four months, had in some ways been dead for the last ten years, was too much for *me* to bear. As sad as dementia was, a part of me envied this man. I wished that I lived in some sort of alternate reality where Eli was just off in surgery for the day and that I expected him home for dinner. How much happier I'd be. That empty hole in my heart wouldn't ache like this if I imagined he was due to be home any moment and not gone from my life.

I followed behind while Matt wheeled his father back to his room and helped him into his bed, adjusting the oxygen tank beside him, and tweaking the bed controls until Maurice was comfortable. Darren, the RN, came in and checked on his patient, and by the time we left, Maurice was dozing, a documentary on the marsupials of Australia on the television.

Matt and I walked out together, passing the young blonde at the front desk who smiled and wished us both a good day.

"I don't know what Dad had against Grandma," Matt confessed as he walked me to my car. "She lived with us for fifteen years. They always seemed to get along fine. Maybe it's just the dementia."

Or maybe his father had been bottling something up that was just now coming to the surface. It must have been difficult, loving your wife and shoving down any bad feelings you had about your mother-in-law. Better to keep it all buried deep than risk hurting your beloved with any criticism of her adored and adoring mother.

Matt stopped at my car. "I visit him every Tuesday and Sunday. If you'd ever like to come along, I know he'd enjoy the extra company."

That might actually be fun. I liked Maurice, and I liked Matt. Anything that got me away from eating a sandwich at my desk while I worked through lunch was a good thing. "Maybe on Tuesdays, unless I've got something urgent at work."

He grinned. "Tuesday, then. Call or text me if you can't make it, otherwise Dad and I will expect you."

I slid into the car. "Thanks again for the help with the furniture and the blankets, and for introducing me to your father. He's a really nice guy."

Matt nodded. "That he is." Then he tapped the top of my car with his palm, gave me a short wave, and headed to his own car.

I headed back to the office, thinking about what Maurice

had said about his wife. There was no mystery, no murder. It seemed like she lived a happy, fulfilling life. She had no reason to haunt a family heirloom. I truly hoped that this was about making sure the sideboard went to a loving home, and that Eleonore would head toward the light in a few days.

Although she might not. If I could only communicate with the ghost, ask her why she was here and what she needed so that she'd be ready to leave. It was easier for those who'd been murdered, but with this ghost, I had no clue. Maybe it was time to call in Daisy's psychic and see if she could give me some answers.

CHAPTER 6

"*This* is Olive O'Toole, and she's a medium."

Daisy had been more excited about the prospect of having a séance in my house than the barbeque this coming weekend. She'd made phone calls, then shown up promptly at six with a short, portly woman whose dark hair was done in what looked like a hundred tiny braids, all gathered on top of her head in a messy bun. Several braids had escaped to stick wildly out of the 'do, reminding me of Medusa.

Olive wasn't the brightly colored scarf wearing, crystal ball toting woman I'd expected. Aside from her dramatic hairstyle, the medium looked like she might be conducting an IRS audit from her tailored navy pantsuit and her glasses.

"Sorry about the clothes," Olive said with a grimace as I waved them into my home. "I just got off work. Usually I'm doing these things at midnight, or at least after dark. I'm not sure how successful we'll be this time of day, but I'll give it a shot."

I'd wanted to have her in early rather than late to avoid disrupting the other resident of my house. In fact, I was really hoping we could wrap this up before Judge Beck got home, to save me from an awkward conversation. I could already imagine how that would go: I see ghosts, and the sideboard I just bought at an auction is haunted, so I brought in a psychic to see what the heck was up with this ghost and if we could convince it to leave.

Yeah. It was bad enough that I'd discovered two murder victims and both times nearly wound up a victim myself without confessing to my new abilities. I considered the judge and his children as my family, and really didn't want to scare them off.

If this didn't work, then maybe I could ask Olive back some evening when the kids were with Heather again and sneak Olive in when the judge was asleep. Or I could tell him we were having some sort of girlfriends' night of wine and cards. And a séance. Because that's what sixty-year-old widows did all the time.

"The sideboard is in here," I said, leading them to the dining room.

"Mind if I scare us up some snacks?" Daisy asked, pointing to the kitchen. I appreciated that she was giving me one-on-one time with her medium friend, as well as thinking about the fact that none of us had most likely eaten since lunch.

"Please do," I told her. She vanished into the kitchen, and I heard the sound of cabinets opening and the clink of glasses and plates.

Olive looked the piece of furniture over, opening drawers and the cabinets, and running her fingers over the surface of the wood while I told her what I knew of its history.

"There's definitely some energy here," she commented. "I can tell that the former owners loved this very much. It could just be a simple attachment that fades over time. How long ago did this Eleonore pass away?"

"Ten years."

Olive grimaced. "That's excessive. If this were a focus piece, then I would have expected her to have moved on after a year or two at the max. Did her husband mention anything about seeing her spirit, or anything unusual associated with it?"

"No, but I didn't ask him." I couldn't imagine asking Maurice Poffenberger if his wife had haunted their dining room furniture, especially with his son Matthew present. "Although I imagine he might have volunteered it if he had seen a ghost. I was asking him about his wife and this piece of furniture in particular, and he seemed open to divulging anything he knew."

She nodded. "It could be that he's not sensitive. I've been in houses swarming with ghosts before and the residents had been happily living there, completely oblivious to their presence."

I winced at the thought of a house swarming with ghosts. One was enough. Two was too many. Swarming would have me calling the realtor and selling the house with the furnishings included.

"So, what's the procedure for something like this? I've never consulted a medium before," I confessed.

She smiled in a warm, friendly, un-psychic fashion and sat down at the dining room table, her hands clasped on top of the table. "First, what are you looking to gain from this visit?"

Ultimately? Get rid of the ghost. This one, not the Eli one.

"Well, I'm curious as to why the ghost is here. Does she want anything? Is there something I can do? Why this sideboard? And then, I'd like her to go away."

Olive nodded. "Daisy said that you've seen spirits of the deceased before?"

"Yes, I have."

I didn't share that fact with a lot of people, and my initial impulse had been to hold as much information back as possible from this medium, to make sure that she was truly communicating with the ghost and not making stuff up. But I trusted that Olive was legit, and not some scammer trying to make a buck with séances and psychic hotlines. I didn't know if it was her businesslike attire, her non-dramatic, professional demeanor, or her fascinating hairstyle, but I trusted her and got the feeling she was legit.

Now, whether she'd be able to sense anything or not was another matter.

"When do you usually see this ghost?" she asked.

I thought for a moment. "Usually whenever I'm in here, or even when I'm walking by the room and happen to glance over. She appears when I'm alone, and once when my room-mate was here. If we're all having dinner, she won't show. She's not here now."

"And you know that she's a she…?"

"I'm not sure. These ghosts are just shadows that seem humanoid in shape. I don't see features or anything that would indicate gender or identity. I just kind of know gender. It's a feeling. As for identity…well, I'm making assumptions there."

She leaned forward and cupped her chin in her hands. "Tell me about the other ghosts that you've seen."

Oh, boy. "Well, this all started after my husband's death and coincided with my cataract surgery. At first, I thought it was some sort of optical side effect of the surgery, but my ophthalmologist says that isn't the case. The first spirit is the one that's here in my house, and occasionally while I'm out and about. He mostly appears during the evenings, and is a comforting presence, sitting beside me. I don't know if it's wishful thinking or not, but I've come to believe that spirit is the ghost of my husband."

"Still a shadow? And he never speaks or performs any poltergeist activity?" she asked.

I shook my head. "He's just there. The other two ghosts I've seen appeared when I discovered the bodies of murder victims. The first only appeared right before I found the body and I think she was playing out the circumstances of her murder. The other one seemed to primarily be in the murdered man's house. He was just present, lurking, although there was one time that he appeared at my work. I got the feeling he was urging me to find his killer."

"It sounds as if the first one was an echo. Those spirits lack consciousness and generally go away within a few days of death, or in this case, when the body was discovered. I think you're right about the other one. Did he vanish once the murderer was discovered?"

I thought for a moment. "No, I still occasionally see him prowling around his yard, or see a shadow in the window of the house."

"He's most likely still connected to his home, which is what I suspect with this one that's haunting your sideboard, although ten years is really unheard of for this kind of haunting. Would you like me to try to contact the other ghost as well? The one who you believe is the spirit of your husband?"

"No." The word was out of my mouth before I could think it. I didn't want to know. I didn't want to feel even more guilty about Eli hanging around, and I especially didn't want to face it if the ghost was someone other than Eli. I mean, that ghost had been in my bedroom many evenings while I was reading or working in my pajamas, propped up on my pillows. The thought that some male ghost other than my husband was hanging out in my bedroom would have been too creepy.

"Okay, then I'll get started as soon as Daisy returns. We'll dim the lights and close the curtains, trying to get it as dark in here as possible. Then we'll all join hands and I'll try to bring the ghost forward. I might need to ask you to request her presence, since she clearly has bonded with you and seems to be shy in the presence of others."

As if on cue, Daisy reappeared, a tray of cheese, crackers, and summer sausage in one hand and a bottle of white wine and three glasses in the other. Taco was following right behind her, meowing and staring up at the contents of the tray as if he hadn't just been fed twenty minutes ago.

"For later," she said, holding up the wine. "I figured after we talk to the ghost, we may need to have a drink. Or two."

Sounded like a plan to me.

Daisy put the food and drinks off to the side of the table, giving me an apologetic smile as she knelt down and slipped Taco a few pieces of cheese and a cracker before she came over and sat down in the chair beside mine. I got up and shooed my cat out of the room, then turned off the lights and pulled the curtains. It did darken the room considerably.

"Candles?" I asked Olive, not sure if we'd need them, or even incense.

"I'm old school," she told me. "I only use candles or incense if they relate to the spirit we're trying to communicate with. In this case, I don't want to scare her off. We're just going to request her presence, be patient, and try to seem as welcoming and non-judgmental as possible."

I sat, and we held hands across the table. Olive began to hum an unfamiliar tune. I closed my eyes and tried to concentrate.

"Can you invite the ghost to join us, Kay?" Olive whispered.

"Eleonore? Or whoever you are? Please come out so we can talk to you." I opened my eyes, but saw nothing by the sideboard. "I love this sideboard. I was so worried that I wouldn't win it bidding at the auction, that it would sell for more than I could afford. I can't tell you how happy I was to bring it home. It looks lovely here. I'll always cherish it, and when I die, I'll make sure it goes to someone who will love it just as much as we both did."

Something shimmered over in the corner, as if there were a sudden wave of heat in that section of the dining room, although the room was quite cool.

"You've shown yourself to me before, and I really would like to see you now. These are friends. You don't need to hide from them."

The shimmer didn't go away, but it didn't coalesce into a ghostly form either.

"You know I love the sideboard. I doubt you've been hanging around for ten years just to make sure it went to a good home. Is there something you want from me? Something I need to do to help you? Because I can't help you if you stay hidden. I can't communicate with you, but Olive can. Please trust her, because if I don't know what you want, I can't help. I want to help. I want your soul to rest in peace."

The shimmer darkened, an inky smudge in a dark corner of an already dark room. Cold brushed my skin and I saw Olive shiver, her grip on my hand tightening. Then her eyes popped open, wide and unfocused.

"I can't rest. I can never rest."

I got the feeling that Olive wasn't Olive right now.

"Who are you?" Daisy asked, clearly with more composure than I had at the idea that a woman in a navy pantsuit was channeling a ghost.

"I can't rest. It was my fault."

I frowned. *What* was her fault? Did Eleonore have a deep dark secret that neither her husband nor her son knew about? From what they'd said about her, she was cheerful and well-loved, but then again, people always tended to exaggerate the good qualities of the dead and forget about their failings.

"What was your fault?" Daisy asked. "Your husband misses you very much."

Olive flinched at that. Then the woman shuddered and drew a deep breath. "I can't rest."

Was everything I'd assumed from my conversation with Maurice and Matt a fabrication? Or had I been making faulty assumptions about something else entirely?

"You son loves you and misses you as well," I told her.

Olive turned blank, confused eyes in my direction. "I can't rest."

"Who are you?" I asked her. "You're not Eleonore, are you?"

She stared at me. "Eleonore?"

I wasn't sure this séance was adding anything but confusion to the situation. If only we could get more than the "I can't rest" on repeat from this ghost. Did she not know the former owner of the sideboard? Who *was* this woman who was haunting my dining room?

"Why are you here?" Clearly the ghost was reluctant or unable to tell me who she was. Hopefully this would be an easier question for her to answer.

"I can't rest."

We'd already established that. "What can I do to help you rest?"

The shadow in the corner of the room changed, becoming more like an image from a very old, damaged photograph. What I saw confirmed that this was a woman, but beyond that, I could make little else out aside from the vague outline of a dress, and a slim hand that rested on the corner of the sideboard.

"No one can help me. I can't rest. It was my fault. I was weak and scared. I didn't know what else to do. I was weak, and it was my fault. May God forgive me for my sins. Please, God, forgive me for my sins. Forgive me for my sins."

I felt cold—colder than I should be, even in the presence of a ghost. The words seared through my mind, jolting my memory. I was thrown back two days, to me sitting at a bingo table next to Matthew Poffenberger, to him telling me of his grandmother.

"Mabel?" I whispered, hardly believing it. If so, then this woman had been haunting the sideboard since 1980, pleading for forgiveness in the company of people who could neither see nor hear her.

"I can't rest," she said one more time. Then the chill and the shadow vanished, and Olive shuddered, returning once more.

I thought back to the picture of Mabel Stevens at nineteen, stunningly beautiful, a socialite and engaged to the most eligible bachelor in the county. Trying to connect her with the puritanical solemn woman of Matt's memory was difficult. Trying to connect both those women to the ghost in my dining room was even more difficult.

It seemed that Maurice Poffenberger was right. His mother-in-law had been wrestling with demons—demons so menacing that she worried God would never forgive her, that she could never rest.

Oh Mabel, you beautiful young girl, what did you do that brought you such pain?

CHAPTER 7

*O*live recovered quickly from her medium activities, and was making a serious dent into the cheese and summer sausage that Daisy had prepared. Daisy and I were the only ones having a glass of wine, since our psychic said that after channeling a spirit, any alcoholic beverage brought on a migraine.

No spirits after the spirit. It made me giggle, which was a clear sign that the night's activity had shaken me to the core.

"That was intense." Olive rubbed her forehead. "That poor woman is wracked with guilt. It's no wonder she's not moved on to her afterlife. I only wish I had been able to find out what she felt guilty about. Many times, I get feelings and impressions from the ghosts beyond what they're verbally communicating, but this time, I was only able to feel her emotions. And they were quite strong. This woman suffered for a very long time, in life as well as in death."

"It's not Eleonore," I told them. "I think that the spirit might her mother, Mabel. The ghost seemed confused at the comment about her son, which would make sense since Mabel only had one child—her daughter. And when you mentioned her husband, she flinched. Eleonore and Maurice had a .very loving relationship from what her son and husband said, but Mabel and her husband's marriage would have frozen water into ice."

"Maybe her guilt is from something to do with her daughter," Daisy conjectured. "Was there any hint that Eleonore's father may have abused her? I can see a mother feeling guilty that she'd not gotten her daughter out of that home, or intervened more forcefully, or something."

I shrugged. "It would be hard for me to research that. He was a prominent businessman in our community. Back then, that sort of thing would have been swept under the rug. Mabel and Eleonore are no longer living, and the only other person who might know would be Maurice, and I'm not sure he'd be willing to talk about that."

"He might talk about it to his son," Daisy suggested. "And in my experience, women who have gone through abuse confide in their friends. None of Mabel's friends are probably still alive, but maybe some of Eleonore's are. Ask her son who his mother's closest and longest female friends are and talk to them."

Daisy had a point. I'd gotten used to doing my research online and sometimes forgot my journalism background.

"Either way, I think it's good of you to dig into this," Olive commented. "That ghost is tormented. She needs help. I'll be happy to come back and try again, or assist in any way that I can because after feeling this woman's sorrow, I can't just ignore her."

I heard a noise, a thump at the door and stood, thinking that Taco was probably trying to headbutt his way to the outside. Maybe if I fed him a second dinner, he'd be quiet. Making my way around Daisy, I nearly collided with Judge Beck.

He stood in the doorway, a huge box in his hands. We

stared at him. He stared at us. From the expression on his face, you would have thought he'd walked in on the three of us dancing naked on the table. Were three women eating cheese and drinking wine all that alarming?

"Um, I'm so sorry," he stammered. "I didn't realize...I'd thought."

Ah, the box. He had come home from the courthouse earlier than I'd expected to spread his files out on the dining room table and work here. I was flattered that he'd rather be in my home, relaxing in the dining room as he reviewed his cases than in his office.

"We're just wrapping things up," Daisy told him. "Olive here just—"

"Came by after work for a visit," I interrupted, shooting Daisy a warning glance. "Go ahead and leave the box and go get yourself something to eat. By the time you've got a sandwich on the plate, we'll have cleared out."

Olive stood at my words, smiling at the judge. Daisy stood as well, but as she had a half-full glass of wine, I knew we'd be moving our "party" to the porch.

"I don't want to displace you ladies," the judge said. "It's your house, Kay. I've been treating your dining room like an office, but you all were here first. I can work upstairs."

I had a vision of him with dozens of files and papers spread all over the bed, and decided that would be rather uncomfortable.

"No, no. It's easier for us to move. We'll go out on the porch. It's a beautiful evening, and Olive and Daisy were just about to leave anyway. Well, Daisy was about to leave once she finished her wine."

Daisy slugged down the wine and sat the glass on the table. "There. Done. I'll take this plate into the kitchen along with the glasses, and the table will be all yours."

I caught the longing in Judge Beck's eyes as he looked at

the leftover cheese and summer sausage. "Just leave the food," I told Daisy.

Olive said her goodbyes, again reiterating that she'd be happy to help if I needed her further. Then she shook hands with Judge Beck, and headed out while Daisy gathered up the wine glasses and scampered into the kitchen. The judge edged around the table to where Olive had been sitting, in front of the sideboard. As he set the box down, he shivered and looked over to the corner of the haunted furniture.

Could he see her? Did he sense her? She'd returned, appearing for the second time with him in the room. Now that she'd made her presence known to Daisy and Olive, would she be less shy? I trusted the spirit I thought of as Eli wouldn't do poltergeist things, but I didn't know this ghost. I wasn't even completely positive who she was.

"Is there a draft?" the judge asked, beginning to pull the folders from the box.

"Possibly. That corner sometimes gets cold." It did, especially since I'd bought that particular piece of furniture.

"I've not met Olive before. Is she a friend of yours from work?"

"She's...she's more Daisy's friend than mine," I replied, realizing that I really didn't have many friends. I needed to invite Carson and Maggie over for dinner. I needed to have Suzette and Kat to Friday wine-on-the-porch again. All I seemed to do was yoga and the occasional happy hour with Daisy. There were so many nights I spent downstairs watching movies, or in the living room trying to knit baby hats for the hospital, or reading up in bed. I relied too much on the judge and his children for company. If I didn't start being more social, developing the friendships I had, then I'd be a very lonely woman when the Beck family eventually moved out.

I guess this weekend's barbeque was just as much about

me getting out of my shell and being social as it was introducing Judge Beck to the neighborhood.

CHAPTER 8

J.T. was in "Gator, Private Eye" mode the next morning, with his arms full of costumes and props for his next video production. I tried to concentrate on the Creditcorp files and ignore him as he went back and forth to the car hauling in stuff, hoping I wasn't going to be roped into this production, either in front of or behind the camera. It wasn't until he brought in an enormous box of Dixie Donuts, trailed by four of our city's finest like he was the Pied Piper of cops that I realized today's production would take place right here in our office. So much for getting any work done.

"We're doing the Mayor Briscane reenactment," one of the cops told me, his grin huge.

That cut really close to home. J.T. always featured real cases, although so far they'd been bail jumpers, repossessions, and the occasional suspected infidelity investigation. This was murder. It was our former mayor. And it was still an open wound for our town, occurring only a few months ago.

"I get to be the mayor and point a gun at you. Don't

worry, it's just a prop gun," the cop added as he turned to pour himself a mug of coffee.

Even worse. I didn't want to relive that. "J.T.?" I called. "Can I have a word with you in private?"

"Can it wait, Kay?" he asked, sitting down his case of camera equipment and flipping the lid open. "I'm paying these guys and don't want them sitting around any longer than necessary."

"Paying us in donuts and coffee," another one of the officers chimed in. They all laughed. Then they all raided the box of donuts like a pack of piranhas.

"Now." I rarely took this tone with my boss, but he knew when I did that I meant business. With a wince, he shut the lid on the equipment box and waved me out front.

I didn't beat around the bush. "It's too soon, J.T. The town is still reeling from the realization that our easy-going mayor is a murderer. Don't do this."

"I'm getting a lot of views, and this case is epic. It's the sort of true crime story that people want to hear, and the fact that this all went down in a small town gives it a huge audience appeal."

It hurt how we'd all been deceived by this psychopath who fooled us into thinking he was an upstanding, moral public servant.

"He was our *mayor*. And before that, he was a county commissioner, and even on the school board. We all trusted him. We all liked him. *You* liked him. He was a friend of yours. You went to breakfast with him regularly, golfed with him. You had dinner at his house with him and his wife."

J.T.'s face hardened at my words, and I realized that his feelings of betrayal were driving this episode of his videocast far more than the lure of additional viewers. This was him lancing an infected wound, removing an offending limb. Pete Briscane had been his friend. J.T. was an investigator, and his friend had been one of the last people he would have suspected of murder. He felt like a fool. He felt betrayed. And this video was his way of cutting Pete from his life and starting to heal.

Who was I to deny someone their recovery? The town wouldn't be wounded any more than the national news attention the case had caused.

"Okay. Fine. But I'm not acting in this and reliving it. I'm not hiding under the desk while that young cop, who looks nothing like Pete, points a gun at me."

"It's a fake gun," J.T. countered.

"I don't care."

"Can you come down to the Megamart this afternoon and—"

"No." I fixed him with my sternest glare. "I'm not reenacting either the discovery of Caryn Swanson's body, or the mayor's murder attempt on me. Either get a stunt double, or film it around me. You might find this whole thing cathartic, but I don't and I'm not doing it."

His expression softened. "Kay, I'm so sorry. I didn't think.... I'm such a jerk. I'm sorry."

"It's okay," I told him. "There's are just some things I don't want to relive. Finding a young woman's body in a watery ditch is one. Thinking that I was about to be killed by our mayor was another."

Add to that finding my neighbor's body and having that murderer try to strangle me. Hopefully J.T. wouldn't decide he needed to add that "case" to his YouTube channel.

"We'll just film it all from a different angle," he told me. "I still want to give you credit for what you did. Honestly, you were the one who did all the investigative work on this case. It's more a Kay, Private Eye than a Gator, Private Eye story."

Kay, because I'd fought hard against any attempts to provide me with a colorful nickname.

"You did plenty, J.T. If it wasn't for you, I'd be dead. You were the one who tackled Pete and subdued him while I cowered under the desk and hoped I didn't get shot."

Suddenly my boss looked every bit of his fifty-eight years old. "That was a fluke. I was supposed to meet Pete for breakfast. If I hadn't swung by the office to grab a file and be late for our meeting, then I wouldn't have been there in time. Maybe you're right, Kay. Maybe I shouldn't do this one."

I took a deep breath. "You should. Pete deserves to have everyone know what a horrible person he was. His victims deserve to have their stories told. I'll deal with it, as long as I don't have to act in this one."

"Deal," J.T. told me. "We better get in there before the all the donuts are gone. Dixie's are the best."

They were, fresh made with local ingredients. "Hope there's a blueberry cream left. And J.T.?" I asked just as he reached the door.

He turned, his eyebrows raised.

"Thanks. For everything. Not just for saving me from getting shot, but for giving me a job when I desperately needed one."

He smiled and draped an arm around my shoulder, ushering me through the door. "I'm happy to have you, Kay," he told me. Then he turned and shouted to the officers clustered around the donut box and the coffee pot, "You guys better have saved Kay one of those, or no one is getting credit in the video."

CHAPTER 9

$\mathcal{I}$ tried to block out the filming of what felt like a major motion picture in my office as I worked. Lunchtime, when the cast and crew were all chowing on pastrami and rye, I called Matt, wanting to know if I could meet him sometime to ask him questions about his grandmother.

I doubted that Mabel was haunting the sideboard out of some need to make sure it went to a loving home, especially given her repeated concerns that she was desperate for forgiveness. What had the woman done? And how long had she been haunting the piece of furniture, desperate for someone to help her find salvation?

Matt sounded thrilled to hear from me, and asked me to meet him after work for a quick cup of coffee at a locally owned shop.

It wasn't until I walked into the coffee shop that I realized he'd again taken my invitation the wrong way. It had been a long time since I'd dated, but I recognized his smile to be a bit warmer and more hopeful than the circumstances allowed for. I'd told him I was a widow. He knew my husband had recently passed, but clearly, he was assuming several communications in one week meant I'd gotten through my grief.

I believe Madison would have announced the situation to be "awk-waaaard". How the heck was I going to wiggle out of this one? And how was I going to ask this man if his mother had been a victim of physical or sexual assault when he thought this meeting was the prelude to a romantic relationship?

I felt even worse when he stood and pulled a chair out for me, asking me what sort of coffee I wanted. I went to tell him that he didn't have to buy me a drink, but there was that look is his eyes again. Hopeful. I'd need to figure out how to let him down gently. Although I was very flattered. The days of men flirting with me were long gone. It was nice to have someone look at me as if I were an attractive woman again. If only this were happening in another two years or so, I might have been more receptive.

"Large dark roast with a splash of cream," I told him. I normally liked my coffee black, but every now and then I liked to mix it up a bit. Cream, or even a spoonful of ice cream, somehow turned coffee from a morning beverage into a festive treat.

"Coming right up." Matt went off to get our drinks while I dug my phone out of my purse and wondered if I should text Daisy.

Yes. Yes, I should.

Help. Asked Matt P to meet me for coffee to ask him more about the ghost, but I think he thinks it's a date.

I held my phone in my lap and watched Matt, hoping Daisy had her phone handy.

My phone chimed. *Awesome! Have fun.*

Thanks a lot, Daisy. I glared at the phone. *It's not a date. I'm a recent widow. I'm not interested.*

Well, have fun anyway. Ooooh—send me a pic. Maybe I'll go out with him if you don't want to.

That was so not going to happen. The pic, I meant, not the dating thing. Although I thought my boss would be crushed if Daisy started to go out with Matthew Poffenberger.

I didn't have time to respond because Matt had returned with our drinks. And two cookies. They were sugar cookies in the shape of butterflies with beautiful iridescent icing on them and little silver dragees at the tips of their antennae.

"Here." He grinned sheepishly. "These were cute. And I don't know about you, but I've got a bit of a sweet tooth."

Oh, I felt terrible. Not knowing what to do, I smiled and thanked him, taking a bite of my cookie and a sip of my coffee.

Well, there was one thing I could say that would totally smash any romantic interest he had, and I was about to do it.

"Remember how I was asking you about the sideboard I bought at your dad's estate auction?" I waited for him to nod. "Well, the reason I've been so interested is that a ghost followed the furniture home, and I was trying to figure out if maybe it was a member of your family, or a former owner of the piece, and why they were haunting it."

He blinked. He didn't run screaming, which was a mixed blessing.

"A ghost? Neither Dad nor Mom mentioned anything about a ghost in our house, and I don't recall seeing or feeling anything. Although maybe none of us are sensitive to paranormal stuff. Or maybe it was someone who owned it before Mom and Grandmother had. How old is it, anyway?"

"They made these styles from eighteen ninety to nineteen twenty," I told him.

"That sideboard came from grandmother, but I don't know who owned it before her. If it's from the nineteenth

69

century, it might have had a previous owner. Grandmother was married in the mid-twenties, but it could have been used when she got it."

"It doesn't bother you that I see ghosts?" Because it was weirding me out that he wasn't weirded out. I'd sort of expected Daisy to take this in stride, but not Matt.

"No. There's all sorts of things that happen in this world that I can't explain. Now if you'd told me that you had vampires living next door, I might have thought differently. But ghosts? Lots of people, normal sane sensible people, see a ghost or two in their lifetime. Can't all be in their heads now, can it?"

Six months ago, I would have said "yes". Well, if the I-see-ghosts thing didn't scare Matt off, this next revelation would.

"Well, since neither your mother nor grandmother had been murdered, I felt like I'd hit a bit of a dead end on figuring out who this ghost was and why they were haunting the sideboard, so I had a friend of mine call in a medium to communicate with the ghost."

He still wasn't running and screaming out of the coffee shop. In fact, Matt leaned forward on the table, obviously fascinated. "What did the medium say? Was there a crystal ball involved? Did the table thump up and down when she contacted the ghost?"

Okay, clearly this guy had watched too many old séance movies.

"No crystal ball or table thumping. Olive came to my house in a smart business suit and didn't even insist on candles or incense. She contacted the ghost, but unfortunately the spirit wouldn't give us her name, and would only repeat a few phrases."

"And it's a woman ghost?" he asked.

"Yes. I can only see a vague, shadow-like figure, but I feel certain this is a woman. Olive said she carries great guilt about something."

Yes, Matt was fascinated. Great. Far from discouraging him, my revelations were somehow making me even more interesting to the guy.

"What did she say? The ghost, I mean."

I took a breath. "She said that she couldn't rest. She kept repeating that over and over again."

"Well, of course she can't rest," he commented. "That's why she's a ghost."

I took a big swig of my coffee, thinking how surreal it was to be having this conversation with Matt.

"She also said that no one could help her, that it was her fault—she was weak and it was her fault."

"Wow, what did she do?" Matt sipped his drink, staring at the table thoughtfully before looking up at me again. "Did she cheat on her husband or something?"

I thought it was odd that Matt immediately went there. Was that the reason that his multiple marriages had ended?

"Or suicide?" Matt added. "Although neither Mom nor Grandmother committed suicide, maybe there was a previous owner of the sideboard who did?"

I hadn't thought of that.

"There's one more thing the ghost said," I added. "She kept saying, 'May God forgive me for my sins. Please God forgive me for my sins. Forgive me my sins.'"

Matt had the same stunned look on his face that I was pretty sure I'd had when the Olive-channeled-ghost had said those words.

"Grandmother?"

"That's what I thought, because I remembered what you and your father had told me about her obsession with being forgiven for her sins."

"But lots of people must say that," he countered. "We've all done things we regret, and depending on our spiritual beliefs, I can imagine many people during their last weeks of life would worry that the mistakes they've made would condemn them to hell."

He had a point. "Most people wouldn't beg for forgiveness over jaywalking or shoplifting, though. It would have to be something big."

"Possibly. I run a therapy group for veterans and first responders. Even the ones who don't have PTSD still have guilt over whether they made the right decisions, constantly second-guessing actions they took for decades. When your split-second decision takes a life, you never really accept that there wouldn't have been another way—whether the person killed was an insurgent or a civilian in the wrong place at the wrong time, or someone on your team that might have lived had you just been a second quicker."

"But neither your mother nor your grandmother served in the military. And if the ghost is someone who owned the sideboard before them, she wouldn't have served, either."

"Actually, she could have. There were many women nurses in World War I, although I think they mostly worked in the rehabilitation centers back home as opposed to on the front line. Maybe she couldn't save one or more of her patients. Maybe she made a bad decision, or didn't take a symptom seriously, and that's always haunted her." He shook his head. "It could have been any number of things."

If I could just nail down who this ghost was, it would be a whole lot easier to find out why she was still lingering after her death. Well, not *easy*, but at least I'd have a place to start research.

Matt took another sip of his coffee. "Or maybe the ghost had an illness toward the end of her life that affected her mentally."

"So, this woman led a blameless life, but due to brain

cancer or something, imagined she'd done something horrible?"

He shrugged. "My grandmother was concerned about her salvation, but from my mother's stories and from what I knew of her, she lived a spotless, admirable life. If you're thinking it's her, then it would have to be an imagined wrong."

"You said she died of a stroke. Did she have something earlier that might have caused her to think she'd done something wrong?"

"No. As far as I know she was very healthy. And she'd always been concerned about her salvation." He frowned. "I can't imagine her having done something wrong, but maybe Dad was right. Maybe she was wrestling with some demons of guilt her whole adult life."

Okay, now *this* was the part where he ran screaming. "Matt, I know your grandmother lived a blameless life, but everyone has secrets. You and your father both noted how much your grandmother loved and cherished your mother. Do you think it would be possible that your mother was the source of her guilt? Maybe she'd been abused as a child, perhaps by her father, and your grandmother hated that she'd not been strong enough to intervene?"

Matt gave me a sideways smile and shook his head. "We can try to ask Dad, but I think you're barking up the wrong tree there, Kay."

"You said your grandfather died before you were born. And with your grandmother still alive, your mother might not have wanted to share that sort of thing with either your father, or with her child. Did she have a best friend, though? Someone she'd known since childhood?"

He sighed. "Mom had always been close with Sarah Hostenfelder. She used to joke that once she married my dad, that they had to stay friends since they both had married into the weirdest names in the town."

Hostenfelder and Poffenberger. And I knew a Hostenfelder—Suzette who'd inherited her grandparents' house at the end of our street. She was in her twenties, so Sarah would have possibly been her grandmother? Or a great aunt?

"What had been Sarah's maiden name?"

Matt frowned for a moment. "Pratt? Yeah, it was Pratt. She was born the same year as my mother and they went to school together. Mom was maid of honor at Sarah's wedding to Josh Hostenfelder. She used to show me the pictures in her album of the wedding. I remember visiting them when I was a kid. They lived in that old German farmhouse at the end of Birch Street, and had a big pond out behind their house."

She had to have been Suzette's grandmother. But if that was the case, then Sarah was also deceased. And it was becoming clear to me that this mystery would never be solved because too much time had passed, and all the people who would have known the secrets had passed as well.

But I had other avenues to explore before I completely threw in the towel on this one. I was convinced the ghost haunting my new sideboard was Mabel Stevens Hansen. And I hoped that there would be some additional clues to dig up, either online, or quite possibly at my friend Suzette's house.

CHAPTER 10

Suzette's eyes lit up when she opened the door and saw the gingerbread cake in my hands. I'd made it for post-yoga breakfast with Daisy tomorrow, but decided it would serve as an appropriate thank you for Suzette lending me her truck, as well as a bit of a bribe for information I hoped to receive. I'd also brought a container of caramelized pears which was probably the most amazing topping that gingerbread ever met. And in case that wasn't enough, I had some whipped cream that I'd made right before coming over.

"Oh, Kay. Bring me food like this and you can borrow my truck anytime. And I don't care what you want to talk about, I'd spill national secrets for that gingerbread. It smells amazing."

I smiled, following her into the house. "Do you know any national secrets?" I could tell that Suzette had been remodeling the old stone and log house that had been built by German immigrants before the Revolution.

"Sorry, no. But I'm happy to tell you anything else."

"I've got questions about your grandmother, Sarah Pratt Hostenfelder. You might not know the answer to them, but

I'm hoping someone in your family does—your father, or maybe one of your aunts or uncles."

Suzette put on a pot of coffee, then pulled two plates and some forks out of the chestnut cabinets. They'd been heavily painted when she'd moved in, but Suzette must have yanked the doors and stripped the four layers of paint and refinished them since then. Slowly the woman was restoring the old house to a modernized version of what it had been two hundred years ago. No wonder I hardly saw her. All she did was work and restore her family home. And as rewarding as I was sure that was, Suzette needed to get out more. She might be young, but there was no reason she couldn't come over for happy hour, or meet me for lunch, or even a dinner.

"I spent a lot of time over here as a kid." Suzette sat across from me and handed me a cake server. "Mom and Dad didn't have money for summer camps or childcare, and we were barely scraping by with both of them working. Mom would drop me by on her way to work, and Dad would pick me up around four when his shift was done. Any school holidays, snow days, even when I was sick, I spent here."

"And your grandfather was strict?" I remembered Daisy saying how Mr. Hostenfelder would always run them off from swimming in the pond when they were kids.

She took the outstretched plate from my hand and spooned a big dollop of warm pears on top of her gingerbread. "Oh, his bark was worse than his bite. The man complained all the time, was as gruff as a bear in winter, but he loved to sit me on his lap and read to me. He's the one who taught me to ride a bike. He and Gran were polar opposites, but they truly loved each other. Icky public displays of affection and all. He died when I was seven."

"And your grandmother was friends with Eleonore Poffenberger?"

Suzette laughed. "Oh my gosh, I haven't heard that name

in ages! She'd been a Hansen, as in the daughter of the department store guy. I was fifteen when she passed away and I went to her funeral with Gran. They were the same age, had been friends forever. They were even in each other's weddings."

"They knew each other since grade school? That's what Matt Poffenberger, Eleonore's son, told me."

"They knew each other before that. Their mothers were very close friends that had grown up together as well. I got the idea Gran and Eleonore rolled around on the same blanket as babies while their moms drank tea and stuff."

I was stunned. Not stunned enough to keep from offering Suzette the whipped cream, but still stunned. "So, your great-grandmother was best friends with, grew up with Mabel Hansen?"

She nodded. "Mabel Stevens before she landed the biggest catch in the county."

Mabel had been best friends with Suzette's great-grand-mother. Their daughters played together, grew up together, were in each other's weddings. But that didn't mean Suzette knew anything about their secrets.

"Did your grandmother mention anything about Eleonore having a secret, or her mother having a secret that they would feel guilty about? Something that would haunt them their whole lives, that they thought was unforgivable?"

Suzette shook her head, then rolled her eyes upward as she stuck a forkful of gingerbread into her mouth. "Holy cow, Kay. This is better than sex. Not that I've had sex in the last two years, but I'm pretty sure from what I remember that this is way better."

I'm wasn't saying my baking wasn't great, but clearly Suzette hadn't met the right man yet.

She swallowed, let out a happy sigh, then ate another bite before continuing. "I never knew Evie, my great-grandmother, but Gran always spoke highly of her as did my grandfather. She was a loyal woman, devoted to her friends and family. She'd do anything for those she cared about. I remember Gran saying that she'd taken care of her friend during her pregnancy, that Eleonore's mom had a rough time of it and had needed to go to the country for fresh air for her last two trimesters. Harlen obviously couldn't leave his business, so Evie took Mabel out to her cousin's home in Pennsylvania until Eleonore was born. Actually, they stayed until Eleonore was about three months old, just to make sure they were healthy enough to come home."

I frowned, wondering why the heck Mabel had needed to go to the country, let alone out of state. Locust Point wasn't a big town now, and it was even smaller back then. I couldn't imagine the air would be any fresher in Pennsylvania than here in 1926.

Maybe she just needed to get away from Harlen. From what Maurice had said, Harlen had been a cold, unloving father. I'd bet he was a cold, unloving husband. Mabel had married the catch of the county; he'd gained a beautiful bride as his trophy, and her pregnancy had been the perfect excuse to get away, at least until she could no longer find an excuse to stay away.

"Did you know anything else about them? I was wondering how Mabel and Harlen's marriage was, if there was any indication that Eleonore's father may have abused her."

"I don't know anything about Mabel and Harlen's marriage, but I'm sure if Eleonore had been abused at all, she would have told my Gran. They knew everything about each other."

"Would she have told *you* any of that?"

"Gran wasn't one for gossip. She talked a lot about her childhood, and her and Eleonore, then about her romance with my grandfather. She had lots of stories, but they were all hers. She wouldn't have told someone else's stories."

Well, that was the end of that.

"I've got the old journals. You could go through them, but from what I read, they're not all that exciting. Mostly they're records of visits, events, and how the tomatoes were looking that year. How many pies she baked, and when laundry day was. That kind of thing."

"Journals? Your grandmother kept a journal?"

Suzette chuckled. "No. If she had, it would have been a far more interesting read. These were Great-grandmother Evie's journals. I kept them because she had descriptions of the house as it was in the early part of the twentieth century. She'd known my grandfather's parents when she was little, and visited a few times and had written about the furnishings and wallpaper and stuff. And I like to keep stuff like that. Makes me feel like I knew the great-grandmother I never met."

"Do you think I could borrow them?"

She nodded. "Of course. As long as I get them back when you're done."

"Wait. How many journals are there?"

"Twenty-five. She'd had one for each year since she was fifteen. Evie died when my grandmother was only nineteen. She was forty when she passed away, otherwise I would have probably had sixty or seventy of them."

Still, twenty-five journals were a lot. I could narrow down certain years, but the secret I was looking for could realistically be in any of them. Or none at all.

CHAPTER 11

"Can I share your workspace?" I asked Judge Beck.

I'd left the rest of the gingerbread with Suzette, inviting her to the barbeque this weekend and returning with my arms full of her great-grandmother's journals. The judge's car was in the driveway, and he was once again sitting at the dining room table, folders and papers spread everywhere. When he looked up at me, I noticed a smudge of ink on the corner of his mouth, as if he'd been chewing a pen. I also noticed something I'd never seen before—the judge was wearing reading glasses.

Reading glasses that he hastily took off when he saw me.

"Don't take those off on my behalf," I told him, setting my laptop and notepad at the end of the table. "Up until my cataract surgery I had a pair of my own. That was one benefit of lens replacement—twenty-twenty vision once more."

He held up the glasses and scowled at them. "I'm too young for these. I don't normally wear them, but if I have a lot of reading, I get eye fatigue and headaches without them."

Too young for those. I hated to tell the judge but most people in their forties did have a pair of cheats.

"Oh, you're just being vain. Wear them if you need. Lots of people do. Besides, you look very handsome with them on."

I don't know why I said the last bit, except that men *were* vain. They dreaded the signs of aging just as much as women did. And he *was* handsome with them on. Of course, Judge Beck was handsome without the glasses, but they gave him an academic serious look that had always appealed to me. Eli, for all his playful sense of humor, had that appeal, especially when he was going over patient files or discussing a tricky surgery.

"Thanks." He reluctantly put them back on and pulled a folder over toward him. "What are you working on?"

Just researching the ghost that's hovering off your left shoulder.

"Some history. A Mabel Stevens Hansen who owned my new sideboard before giving it to her daughter, Eleonore Hansen Poffenberger, as a wedding gift."

The judge blinked. "Hansen, as in Harlen Hansen, the owner of the department store?"

"The very same. Do you know anything about him or his family?"

"Not beyond the fact that he was rich, well respected, and the owner of a successful store. I'm not a local, Kay. I moved to Milford twenty-five years ago, and we didn't come to Locust Point until after Madison was born. I do know that Hansen was a big donor to the local police. There's a plaque recognizing something he did over at the courthouse. I think he was pretty close with one of the judges at the time, too."

"How do you know that?" I put the stack of journals on a chair next to me, thinking it would be really cool if I could get a hold of journals from a judge back in the twenties.

"There's a hallway in the courthouse with pictures of all the former judges, the ribbon cutting from when the new courthouse was built, and some drawings and photos of the old courthouse before it burned down. There's one of Judge Rickers and Harlen Hansen shaking hands, and they just have that look about them, as if it wasn't just a formal picture. They look like old friends."

That wasn't too surprising. Harlen was a wealthy local businessman, and Locust Point was a small town. If everyone knew everyone else's business now, I was pretty sure it was the same back then. Just as my boss had been buddies with our former mayor, I could see the judges back then being friends with Harlen Hansen.

Of course, J.T. hadn't known his buddy the mayor was a murderer. If Harlen was an abuser, it would also be possible that his judge friend knew nothing about what happened in Harlen's home.

I wasn't ready to open up to Judge Beck about the ghosts, but I'd learned that he had good intuition and insight as far as people and motivation went. I needed a fresh perspective —someone who wasn't related to either Eleonore or Mabel or their friends. He might have been busy with the files spread all over the table, but he seemed open to taking a bit of a break. Hopefully he could provide an ah-ha moment of perception that would shed light on why this ghost was hanging around.

"Mabel Stevens Hansen, Harlen's wife, felt very guilty about something she'd done. She loved her daughter very much, and people tell me that Harlen was very cold and distant toward the pair of them. I wonder if he didn't abuse the daughter and she never forgave herself for not stepping in, or protecting her child. I'm hoping her friend might have noted it in her journals, but wondered what you thought about that theory. Would something like that cause enough guilt to…. well, to haunt someone for the rest of their life?"

Judge Beck gave me an odd look. "I see a lot of domestic violence cases, and what drives many women to press charges and leave an abusive marriage is when it starts happening to the kids. There are a few cases where the woman feels so trapped she stays, sometimes even convincing herself it's the child's fault, or that the kid is making it all up, but in those cases, there's usually a lot of animosity and blame between the child and both her parents. If Mabel and her daughter were close and loving, then I don't think her turning the other way to abuse was the cause of her guilt."

"Maybe she successfully intervened, which is why Harlen was so distant to them. And she regretted that it ever happened. And Eleonore loved her mother because she knew the woman stood up for her against her older, more powerful husband." I was grasping at straws, but something in my gut told me that Mabel's torment had something to do with Eleonore.

"Back then, Harlen would have held a lot of power in the marriage. There wouldn't be much Mabel could have done beyond leaving him, and *that* would have been a huge public scandal. She either left, or she stayed and swept it under the rug, or he wasn't abusive at all."

"But he wasn't affectionate," I argued. "He barely spoke to them. He hardly spent any time with them outside of at dinner."

"Some men aren't physically demonstrative, Kay. And back then, there was a ridiculous social standard that men be the strong breadwinners while women were the nurturers and homemakers." He grimaced. "I'm dealing with that myself. I was gone all the time, working insane hours to build a stable career to provide for our family, where Heather was a stay-at-home mom who made sure everything behind the scenes ran smoothly. I'm sure I seemed distant and uninvolved a lot of the time, because I was. I was barely able to keep up with what was happening at the law firm, and then at the courthouse, let alone know what sports the kids had which night, whether they had a math test the next day, or who was doing what for their science fair project."

"I see you with Madison and Henry, and you are far from cold and distant," I protested. "You might have been uninformed, might not have known the details of their schedules and their activities, but I can tell you've always shown affection toward them."

"A kiss goodnight when they've already been asleep an hour isn't enough—for a child or a parent. I resented it." His voice grew gruff. "I envied Heather getting to see all those special moments, getting to put bandages on skinned knees and bribing the kids to eat their carrots. That resentment made me pull away from them even more. I retreated into my work, hating this bargain we'd made, but not knowing how to turn it around. I missed my children's childhood, and no amount of money and career success makes up for that."

How did we go from Harlen Hansen to the judge's personal life? This was the first he'd really gotten into the details of his crumbled marriage with me. I knew what a private man he was, and even though we were off topic, I was pleased he considered me enough of a friend to confide these things to me.

"My father was a cop. I know all about that kiss in the middle of the night. And no matter how much adults tried to hide it, I knew in my heart there was always a chance that he might not come home from work at all. Yes, Mom was the one at all my parent-teacher conferences, the one baking cookies for teacher appreciation day and taking me to the park, but I adored my father and knew how much he loved me, even though his schedule meant he wasn't around much."

Judge Beck took off his glasses and rubbed his face. "I know my kids probably understand just as you did, but that doesn't mean *I* didn't resent it. I blamed Heather, and I still kind of do blame her. I worked these insane hours, then I'd come home and she'd be chatting on the phone with her friends, making plans for play dates at the country club pool and arranging for a sitter so she could meet them for lunch. After a while, I felt like I was just a paycheck to her. I felt like the only purpose I served for my family was to bring home money. When we'd gotten married, it seemed like the right thing to do. I made more than she did. My career had more potential than hers. She wanted to stay home with the kids, and it was unheard of for a man to do the same. But as the years went on, I began to feel like she got the best end of that deal."

"Yes, but you're changing that," I told him softly, resisting the urge to reach out and take his hand. "I know trying to juggle both your career and parenting is exhausting, but you're finally able to spend time with your children. You changed that dynamic."

He grimaced. "Heather changed that dynamic. I was trying to get more regular hours, to make time to go to the kids' games and do family things on weekends as opposed to being locked in my office, but it seemed like the more time I spent at home, the more we fought. Then she dropped the divorce bombshell."

Oh, my heart ached for him. As much animosity as he and Heather had for each other, I could tell he still loved his wife, and that there was still something in her heart for him. Was it just the longing, the memories of what they'd had before? Was their love so dead that there was no hope that it could rise again, like a phoenix from the ashes?

"Maybe Mabel cheated on Harlen," Judge Beck said, his voice bitter. "Trust me, that's a hard thing for a man to take. And back then, a divorce would have been humiliating. Bringing the fact that he was a cuckold to light would have been tough for a successful, prominent man like Harlen Hansen."

I winced. Then I asked something that was absolutely none of my business.

"Did Heather cheat on you? I heard you mention someone named Tyler before."

He hesitated a moment, then sighed. "I had a private investigator follow her, not that infidelity means much in today's no-fault divorce proceedings, but I thought it might help with the custody case. They couldn't find any evidence that she'd been sleeping with Tyler prior to filing for divorce, but their relationship clearly didn't come out of nowhere. Tyler has a son Henry's age, and he's a single dad. They were at a lot of school events together, on several fund-raising committees. There was an affection there. And while there might not have been any physical infidelity that I could prove, I'm certain there was emotional infidelity."

And that hurt just as much. He admitted he'd been distant and uninvolved, and Tyler evidently had stepped up to the plate in his stead. But this had been the agreement he and Heather had made between them, the division of roles. Had she expressed her dissatisfaction with those roles before Tyler was in the picture? When Judge Beck decided to try to change things, was it just too late to revive what they'd once had?

He shook his head. "She suspected the same about me. I found out she'd hired someone a year before she asked for a divorce to follow me around and make sure I really was working those late nights and not heading off to a hotel with some woman. She'd accused me of that before, but now I wonder if it was just wishful thinking on her part—her hoping that I'd give her an excuse to ask for a divorce without looking like the villain."

"Did you ever cheat on her?" I asked, just to be fair.

"No. There were a few times I was tempted. When you work long hours and feel like a stranger to your own family, it's difficult to not be drawn to that person who shares your passion for your career, who you think truly *gets* you. But I know that's an illusion, and a coward's way out. I came very close a year ago, and that's when I decided I needed to look long and hard at my priorities and my work schedule, to stop being bitter about the roles in our marriage and work actively to change them into something that would make me happy. I guess I was too late."

"I'm so sorry," I told him.

He shrugged and put his glasses back on, pulling a folder over in front of him. "It hurts. I'm not the first to survive a painful divorce, and I doubt I'll be the last. My goal now is to make sure everything works out the best it can for Madison and Henry."

He'd tried to make a change. Even if he was too late to save his marriage, it wasn't too late to be an active and involved parent to his kids. And for that I truly admired Judge Beck.

I watched him for a second, then turned my thoughts back to the ghost standing off in the corner of the room. If infidelity had broken apart Harlen and Mabel's marriage, it had most likely happened after Eleonore was born. And Harlen didn't strike me as the sort of man who would forgive that.

Were the judge and Matt right? Had a young, beautiful Mabel strayed from her marriage? Was that what made her beg for forgiveness? I looked up at the ghost in the corner of the room and wished I could see her better, wished she could talk to me and tell me what made her linger here after death. But there was something off in my theory. Harlen might have never forgiven Mabel for having an affair, but he wouldn't have taken it out on Eleonore, his only child. And from the timing, Mabel had become pregnant soon after her marriage, when she would be unlikely to have had an affair.

Hopefully the answer would be in Evie's diaries. I looked at the stack of faded books I'd put on a dining room chair and pulled the first one to me. It was dated 1920 in an elegant swirling script. Evie would have been fifteen, and Mabel thirteen.

An hour in, and I was ready to throw the book through the window. Reading Evie's handwriting was difficult enough, but she tended to use initials and documented the most mundane and boring events. I did find out that she was eagerly anticipating her sweet sixteen party, and that MS would be invited, even though Evie was a bit worried that MS's beauty would catch the eye of HP, whose tall straight form and kind eyes she greatly admired. I finished out the 1920 diary, deciding that I knew far too much about Evie's menstrual cycles, which she marked with a little circle, and her practiced arguments to sway her parents into allowing her to cut her hair in a more fashionable style. At the end of the year, Evie had turned sixteen, Mabel was now fourteen, and Evie's hair was still long and braided "like the elderly ladies wore".

I skipped ahead four years, figuring that I might find out more when Mabel was older. That put Evie at nineteen and Mabel at seventeen when the journal started. Evie had finally gotten the haircut she'd so wanted, but she now lamented that her thick, coarse hair wasn't so easy to tame at a shorter length. She openly admired MS's shiny, fine black locks that waved perfectly around her beautiful face, and expressed gratitude that her friend was not the sort of girl who would steal HP's affections away with her good looks—not at all like her sister LS.

That was right. Mabel had a twin, an equally beautiful twin, who seemed to vanish around the time of her marriage.

I'd assumed Lucille had married beneath her and that the controlling Harlen hadn't allowed them to associate, but now I wondered. Matt hadn't known about his great aunt Lucille so perhaps she'd died young, and it had been her passing away and not Mabel's stern husband that explained the lack of mention. I made a note on my pad of paper to look through death notices, wincing at the fact that I might need to dig through twenty years of them to find out when Lucille died.

Clearly, she was alive at this point in 1924 when Evie was increasingly in love with the man who I assumed was Howard Pratt—her future husband. Lucille was equal in beauty to Mabel, but according to Evie, a flirt. I began to stay alert for any future mentions of LS, and was surprised to see that there weren't many of them. Didn't twins tend to hang out together? Have the same group of friends? I wasn't really sure, having been an only child myself, but I imagined sisters would be close enough that they'd hang in the same social circles.

By the end of 1924, it became clear to me that as close as Evie was to Mabel, she truly disliked Lucille, who in round-about terms she described as a flirt and a wild, immoral girl.

I might not have had a sister, but I was a woman and I knew how girls could be, so I took all this with a giant boulder of salt. It was clear that Evie didn't consider herself a beautiful woman in the norms of the time. Mabel was beautiful, but was kind and quiet and somewhat shy, so she wasn't seen as a threat. Lucille wasn't shy, from what I could tell as I delved into 1925. She snuck out and went to parties where there was alcohol and dancing, where she smoked cigarettes and associated with colored folk and came home late or sometimes not at all. MS had fretted about her sister's safety and reputation, and Evie worried that Lucille's wild ways would reflect poorly on her friend.

But this was only one side of the story, and Suzette had said both Evie and her daughter Sarah were incredibly loyal people. Could it be that Evie was making Mabel into the saint she wasn't, and painting her sister a far more sinister shade than she deserved? I was sure envy had something to do with her opinions. Mabel was her shy friend, where Evie not only turned all the boys' heads, she encouraged their attentions. Had Howard once cared for Lucille? Because I'd seen more than once how jealousy could cloud a person's judgment.

Then I turned the page and caught my breath. Evie's journal entries were all carefully worded and coded, because she was trying not to be a despicable gossip, but the woman was clearly upset, and for once had spelled everything out.

"What?" Judge Beck asked me. He'd been eyeing me occasionally as we worked, clearly curious about what I was reading.

"Lucille, Mabel's twin sister. She was caught in a rather compromising position with a married man by the police chief. He told her father, and she was kicked out of their home. Her father put her on the street with a bag of clothes and told her never to come home, never to speak to him again."

The judge winced. "That seems rather harsh."

It was, but Lucille's partying and drinking and smoking and dancing must have set the stage for this straw that broke her father's back. And from what I'd read, he'd had a lot to lose. Mabel was expecting a proposal from Harlen any day, and this scandal with her sister might have put that alliance in jeopardy.

But to put his own daughter out on the street? "I thought people sent their children away to visit relatives out of state when that kind of thing happened, not kicked them to the curb."

I was getting an idea of what happened to Lucille. That must have been when she'd vanished from Mabel's life. Had she run off with her married lover to live in sin somewhere, disowned by her family? Was that the guilt Mabel carried? Did she wish that after all those years she'd reached out to her sister? Had Lucille died before a reconciliation could happen, and Mabel regretted not extending the olive branch sooner?

But the ghost had made it sound like the guilt was from something *she'd* done. And while I could see asking for forgiveness—both of her sister and of God—for not reuniting before it was too late, I couldn't imagine this was what would drive Mabel to haunt a piece of furniture for decades after her death. It wasn't like she was the one who'd kicked Lucille out of the house. It wasn't like she'd forced her wild sister into the arms of a married man.

"You said this was around 1920? Loose behavior was still a stigma, but I'm sure with the changing social norms, Lucille found friends to take her in," the judge commented, a frown on his face.

I made another note on my paper. Try to find out Lucille's date of death, although that might be difficult if she'd left the county, and see if there was any note of who she may have moved in with.

"Would there be a record if this married man left his wife for Lucille?" I asked the judge. "I know a lot of records were lost in the courthouse fire, but was that sort of thing reported in the paper?"

"The courthouse fire was before that, and most of the records were preserved off site since they were outgrowing that building by that time. And yes, there would be a record, and such a scandal would have made the papers unless her family had the money to squash the story. Even if the man hadn't filed for divorce, his wife would have filed for abandonment."

I made another note. "Are those records online?"

"Not those. We microfiched all the records back in the seventies and eighties, but only bothered to put the last twenty years of records in an electronic format. You'll need to go into Milford. And it will take some time unless you know exactly when the man or his wife would have filed. Or even their names." He shook his head. "You're better off checking the paper first. They've archived everything electronically and it's all available online. Milford County Historical Society had a series of fundraisers to pay for it all as part of their preservation project."

I grimaced. "Mabel was expecting a proposal from Harlen Hansen right about then. I know her family wasn't well connected, but there's a chance the whole story wouldn't have seen the light of day."

"Not necessarily. If the gossip was public knowledge, then there wouldn't be much they could do. Plus, I don't know if the society and gossip columnists would be easily silenced about something like that. Harlen Hansen driving drunk into a light pole—that they may have hushed up and not reported. Harlen Hansen's almost fiancée's sister being caught by the chief of police with her skirts up in the company of a married man would have been gleefully reported."

He was right. And the paper would have been more than happy if Harlen had broken things off with Mabel and gone back to being the county's most eligible bachelor. But he hadn't broken things off. In spite of his reputation, had he really loved Mabel? Loved her enough to overlook a wild twin that most likely ran off with her lover?

I wasn't particularly tired, but it was late and I had an early morning tomorrow with Daisy's and my sunrise yoga, then work. So I slid a bookmark into the journal, hoping that

Evie documented what had happened to the prodigal Stevens sister, wished Judge Beck a good night, and headed upstairs to lie in bed, wide awake with all the drama of nearly one hundred years ago running through my head.

A shadow formed in my peripheral vision and sat in the lounge chair, this one a welcome visitor to my bedroom.

"What do you think, Eli?" I asked the ghost. "Have I been wrong? Maybe Mabel's guilt isn't something to do with her daughter, or with her marriage to Harlen. Maybe it's about her sister." I thought once more of Lucille. She'd been disowned. If she'd run off with her lover, only to have him ditch her, what would she have done? It had been late 1925 and women without any family connections, women who'd been tossed from their home for sleeping with a married man wouldn't have had many opportunities in terms of a job or ways to support herself. Had she come back and asked Mabel for help? Had her sister refused, or been pressured to refuse, driving a wedge between husband and wife and causing Mabel's guilt? If they'd turned Lucille away, and the woman had been forced into prostitution to support herself, perhaps even dying young because of it, wouldn't that be enough to cause Mabel to beg the Lord for forgiveness of her sins?

Yes, it would. But in order to know what really happened, I'd need to discover what happened with Lucille.

CHAPTER 12

"*J*'m so angry about that young woman's father kicking her out," Daisy sputtered. "I could do sun salutations all day long, and I'd still be furious. How could anyone do such a thing and call himself a parent? And where was that girl's mother? Because she should have taken a frying pan to her husband's head."

"She died when the girls were about five. And I'm not defending him at all, but Lucille sounds like a wild child. She was eighteen and sneaking out of her home, drinking and smoking, and evidently screwing around with a married guy. It wasn't like they had a military school for girls to ship her off to, and she was eighteen anyway. We don't know how many warnings he gave her, or if he told her he'd kick her out the next time, or what. All we have is Evie's note in her journal."

"And Evie clearly didn't like Lucille." Daisy glared at me, as if I were the one who had turned a young woman out onto the streets. "What if that guy had raped her and no one believed her? What if he'd gotten her drunk, or slipped her something? And why isn't he in the gutter with his bag in hand? He's the one breaking marriage vows, not Lucille."

"I know, I know," I assured her. "I hate it too, but this was over ninety years ago, Daisy. We can't do anything about it now. Maybe there weren't shelters and places to help women in those situations then like there are today."

"There aren't nearly enough of them even today," she grumbled.

I knew that Daisy worked with young at-risk girls, that she probably saw more than her fair share of rape victims, homelessness, and wrongful blame. It made me even more determined to find out what happened to Lucille.

"And why didn't her sister stand up for her?" Daisy demanded. "If my father had kicked my twin out of the house, I would have gone to that rich influential guy who supposedly was on the verge of proposing and asked him to at least make sure my sister had the resources to live independently and not starve to death."

I hadn't thought of that. Evie had described Mabel as kind, shy, and reserved. Maurice had described her as strict and unbending. Which was right? Had the woman changed that much over her life? Perhaps Mabel had gone to Harlen and promised to marry him if he helped her sister, although from what Evie had implied in her journals, Mabel was set on marrying him anyway.

"Let me dig a little and find out what happened," I told Daisy. "I'll tell you what I find out. For all we know, Mabel sent her a check every month to help her out. For all we know, the married guy left his wife, ran off with Lucille, and the two of them lived in sin happily ever after."

"I hope so," Daisy said as she rolled up her mat. "I hope that Lucille had her happily ever after and didn't end up having to turn to prostitution to make ends meet, or died from starvation in an alleyway somewhere."

I hoped so as well, but that ghost in my dining room made me fear that Lucille hadn't had her happy ending.

* * *

J.T. HAD me researching some potential bail clients from Milford, so I wasn't able to get to the Stevens's family drama until late in the day. Since I had a date for the married-man-scandal, it was fairly easy to find in the newspaper archives—and it was there, in the social column, with as many lurid details as were probably permissible to print back then.

The police chief had heard some noise in a small public park downtown and gone to investigate. There he found Silas Albright seated against a tree, pants down to his ankles, with a woman straddling him, her skirt around her waist. It had been night, but she'd turned slightly when the chief had called out, and he'd recognized her. Silas had done the only gallant act of the evening, pushing Lucille off and behind him as he stood, pants still around his ankles. Then he confronted the chief, ensuring that Lucille could slip away, and refused to name her.

I was flabbergasted. No one had known besides the two lovers and the police chief. If that big jerk had just kept his yap shut, nobody else would ever have known about it. If the chief had really been so appalled at the immorality of the two, he could have taken Lucille aside privately and warned her about the possible consequences of her actions. She was not even nineteen yet. An eighteen-year-old girl. And I had no idea how old Silas Albright was, but maybe the chief should have scolded him about public exposure and honoring the sanctity of his marriage vows as well. Then he could have gone home to his own wife, and let it all go.

No. He'd gone to his buddy and told him what he'd seen. And Lucille's father had kicked her out of the house, yelling at her while Mabel stood by and cried, the whole neighbor-hood witnessing the spectacle. He hadn't done it to protect Mabel's reputation, or potential engagement to Harlen Hansen, he'd done it because he was angry at his daughter. And instead of doing it quietly and keeping everything hush-hush to preserve reputations, he'd branded her a loose woman in front of the entire neighborhood.

Daisy was right. This guy was the worst sort of human being. And now I really *was* concerned about Lucille. A young woman, out on the streets alone. With the story splashed all over the town, would even her friends have taken her in? And Silas…. Yes, he'd cheated on his wife, and I wasn't at all excusing him for that, but he'd also tried to shield Lucille and refused to name her. He'd taken the heat with the chief, and tried to keep a young woman's reputation intact.

I hated this police chief. And I hated Hugh Stevens. Both had died long before I was born, but I still wanted to drive down to the cemetery and spit on their graves.

In spite of searching until well after quitting time, I couldn't find anything further on Lucille or Silas. The 'inci-dent' had occurred in October of 1925. The girls had turned nineteen in December. Mabel's engagement announcement was in the paper in January with a June wedding planned. I gathered up some files to take home with me. Then just before I left, I checked one more thing.

The Stevens-Hansen wedding had taken place June 2, 1926, as planned. There was a picture of a stern Harlen with his bushy mustache and potbelly standing next to a beautiful Mabel. The bride had a beaded sheath dress with a stylish handkerchief hem, a beaded headdress accessorizing the beautiful, wavy, jaw-length bob that Evie had so envied. But it was her eyes that caught my notice. Earlier society pictures of Mabel had shown a sweet, happy beauty. This picture showed a beautiful woman, but one who looked more like she was at a funeral than her wedding.

It wasn't until I'd gotten home and settled in a comfy armchair with several of Evie's journals and cup of hot tea that it hit me. Mabel was married in June of 1926 at the age of nineteen. Her daughter, Eleonore, was born in December of 1926. Either Mabel had given birth to a very premature six-month fetus, or she'd been pregnant at the time of her wedding.

A pregnant woman would need to get married, especially after she'd just seen what her father had done to her sister. Either Harlen had jumped the gun and decided that an engagement ring was sufficient promise for him to begin intimate relations with his intended, or Mabel had gotten pregnant by another man.

And if she had, Harlen would have done the math just as easily as I had. And he would have been cold and resentful of both his wife and the daughter he had to raise as his own. Judge Beck was right, except Mabel hadn't cheated on her wedding vows—she'd deceived her fiancé into marrying a woman pregnant with another man's baby.

If that was the case, then Mabel was more like her twin than her friend Evie had thought.

CHAPTER 13

"*Makes* sense," Judge Beck said, offering me another piece of pizza. It was a risky dinner for us to be sharing, given that the dining room table was covered with his paperwork and Evie's journals. As glad as I was that he'd brought home food, I was wishing it was something less messy. "Although I'd rather think that Harlen consummated his marriage before the vows than believe that his fiancée was running around on him."

"Did people really do that?" I asked, licking sauce off one of my fingers. "Consider engagement as good as a wedding vow, I mean, not cheat on their fiancés."

"Yeah to both. The latter means that Mabel wasn't that nice, sweet girl that her friend thought she was. Cheating on your fiancé and trying to pass off another man's kid as your husband's is pretty reprehensible in my eyes."

In mine too, and I just couldn't see the Mabel from Evie's journals doing that. But I was only getting Evie's view of the woman.

"Maybe Mabel came clean to Harlen before their marriage and he stepped up to the plate and helped her out?"

I conjectured. It didn't seem in keeping with his reputation, but at least it would make Mabel less of a horrible woman.

The judge shrugged. "If he was really obsessed with her, he might have married her anyway, then when the glow faded, he ended up resenting that he was stuck raising another's child as his own and with a woman who'd married him to save her reputation."

"Or for his money," I suggested. "If she was pregnant by someone else, then why hadn't she run off and marry that guy? Given what I've learned about her, I'm thinking she probably loved the man if she was sleeping with him. The only reason to stay and marry Harlen instead was that she wanted the money and status that went along with being his wife."

Which would be so cold. Evie was most likely painting a glossy picture of her friend, but how could sweet, loyal Mabel leave the man she loved and deceive another just for money and social status? Had her sister's plight frightened her? Was she worried that she'd wind up like Lucille if she didn't marry the man her father wanted her to marry?

And what had happened to Lucille after getting tossed out of her home?

"Maybe the father of her child was a jerk and didn't want to marry her. Or maybe Lucille wasn't the only one having sex with a married man."

I winced, thinking that Judge Beck could be right. Deceiver. A party to adultery. Money-grubbing. None of these were things I wanted to believe about Mabel. I shook my head, thinking that Mabel's motives might be something we never discovered. "What I don't understand is how they could have kept Eleonore's actual birth date a secret. It was correct on the county death certificate that I saw. I couldn't find a birth certificate online, but I just assumed it was too old to be scanned in, or that it had been lost."

"Maybe because she'd had the baby out of state?" Judge Beck guessed. "Birth certificates weren't as big a deal then as they are now. You could go through your whole life and not need one for anything. Heck, lots of rural people with home births didn't even have a birth certificate. The family bible was accepted as a record of birth date, death date, and wedding date in most counties. If she had the baby in Pennsylvania and stayed there for a few months, she could have just announced the birth as later than it truly was."

The society pages had not been abuzz with Eleonore's early birth. Mabel *had* given birth out of state and the announcement hadn't shown up in the paper until March— claiming the baby was born in March 1927. Then the three-month-old baby that arrived home was actually a six-month-old baby. Throughout it all, Evie, pregnant herself, had helped Mabel stay away as long as possible to keep the deception. Evie had lived apart from the husband she'd loved for nine months to help her friend.

But had Harlen been fooled? It was unlikely given how he'd treated both his wife and daughter going forward. But he hadn't kicked them out—no doubt saving himself the humiliation of letting the world know he'd been suckered into marrying a woman pregnant with another's child. It was doubtful that he'd have let his young, beautiful wife remain in the country from September of 1926 to June of 1927 without visiting her. Mabel was a slim, petite woman. Even with a first pregnancy, she would have clearly been a trimester further along than she should have been.

"So, Mabel heads out of town before she gets too big, claiming she's having a rough pregnancy. She has a baby in December. Makes the announcement in March, when she should have had the baby. Gets a faked birth certificate if she needs one, then comes back to Locust Point in June with a baby that's actually three months older than anyone thinks."

I was pretty sure some of the experienced moms would have suspected, but all Mabel had to do was claim continued poor health and concern over the health of her baby, then keep most visitors away until the baby was old enough to pass for the age she claimed it was.

But Evie had known. At the end of the 1925 journal, she was engaged to Howard Pratt. She'd exchanged vows with him in January in a whirlwind marriage, and she'd also given birth in December of 1926, out of state with her friend. The two girls had grown up together, and at some point, the actual date of Eleonore's birth had come out because Suzette made it clear that her grandmother and Eleonore were the same age, both born in 1926, not 1927 as Mabel had no doubt told the town.

Eleonore at some point had found out the truth about her birthdate. And she'd most likely had done the math as well. What had she thought about her parentage? Had she ever asked her mother?

It was something I needed to ask Matt and possibly his father about.

"Sounds like this Mabel had a lot to feel guilty about," Judge Beck commented as he grabbed another slice of pizza.

I nodded. She did. But there was so much more I needed to find out. Who was Eleonore's father? Had Mabel really been as materialistic as I was thinking, or had she been a scared, panicked young woman who felt she had no other options? And what had happened to Lucille?

I kept reading Evie's journals, my vision blurring with the huge entries that detailed her wedding dress, how handsome Howard looked, and who was at the wedding. There were a few missed journal entries the days after their marriage that prompted a knowing smile from me. Yes, Evie had loved Howard, and it was very obvious that they were keeping each other too busy for lengthy journal entries. For the first few months of 1926, there was little mention of Mabel and none of Lucille as Evie waxed poetic about married bliss.

Then in June, I read something that had me reeling. Right before Mabel's extravagant wedding to Harlen—the day before, in fact—Lucille's body had been found floating in the Hostenfelder pond.

I choked back a sob, tears in my eyes as I put the journal down, needing a break. Actually, I needed a glass of wine and a good cry.

"What? What happened?" Judge Beck's brows came together in worry. "I swear I'm getting attached to these people of yours. I'm far more interested in what's going on with Evie, Mabel, and Lucille than this vandalism case."

"Lucille is dead. Facedown in the Hostenfelder pond the day before Mabel's wedding," I told him, feeling a bit foolish, like I was about to cry over a fictional soap opera character or something. These people were all long dead, but over the last few days, I'd become so invested in their lives that reading the shocking announcement in Evie's journal gutted me.

Swimming accidents did happen, but I could tell from the expression on Judge Beck's face that he was thinking the same thing that I was.

"That's horrible," he said in a hushed tone. "Kicked out of her father's house, probably spurned by her married lover and denied help from those who had been her friends and family."

"She takes her own life," I completed the thought. "And the timing of it can't be a coincidence. Did Mabel turn her away a few days before her wedding, fearing that Harlen might call things off if she helped her scandalous sister?"

"Mabel was pregnant. She had to marry someone, and Harlen was probably in a better position to provide for her than any other man. Plus, if he called the wedding off, she wouldn't have time to get engaged and marry another man before she started showing."

"And if a three-month-early baby was a tough story to pull off, then a six month one, or even a bride nine months pregnant would have been impossible. She would have had to sneak out of state, have the baby in secret and give it away, then come back as if it never happened."

"Which wouldn't have been an option. If the father kicked Lucille out for being involved with a married man, then he would have done the same to Mabel for getting pregnant out of wedlock. There would have been no sneaking away to the country and secret adoption for her. She would have found herself out in the street just like her sister, only pregnant."

"So, she turned her sister away to save herself," I mused. "Although, to be fair, maybe she intended on helping her sister later, after everything was settled with Harlen and she'd had the baby."

"Maybe Lucille didn't have the time to wait," the judge suggested. "Suppose she was pregnant as well, maybe even three months further along. A six-month pregnant woman would need help now. Although I'm not sure how Mabel could have helped her. It wasn't like she had money of her own."

"No, but she probably had a spending account for the wedding. How hard would it have been to divert some money for her sister? Just enough for her to rent a cheap apartment in Milford and eat."

"I'll bet both her father and Harlen had a tight grip on the money, though. Her father had to have suspected that Lucille might come to her twin for help. And a businessman like Harlen might want to keep an eye on the wedding expenditures as well."

"Poor Lucille." And poor Mabel. Two girls in trouble. One takes her life, the other condemns herself to a loveless marriage to ensure her baby has the best life possible. If only Lucille hadn't been caught. If only that stupid police chief had kept his mouth shut. Then maybe Lucille could have found a way out of her problems that didn't involve drowning herself in a pond.

"There's your guilt. Mabel felt responsible for her sister's suicide. That must have been hanging over her for her entire life." Judge Beck shook his head. "I kind of wish Madison was here right now, because I feel the urge to hug her tight and tell her that I love her, tell her that no matter how hopeless things seem, I'm always here to help. I might yell at her first, but I'll always help."

I thought back on the Caryn Swanson murder, when I'd found out that Madison had attended a party with older kids, drinking and unwittingly hanging with girls who had been involved in a prostitution ring. Judge Beck had been furious at his daughter, but even then, I'd known that anger came from fear for her wellbeing and from love.

"I can tell you're thinking of saying 'no' to her proposed movie date with Austin Meadows," I told him, trying to lighten the mood a bit.

"I want to, but I won't. I'd rather she come to her mother and me than sneak around behind our backs. Besides, this way I can have a little chat with Austin Meadows before their date."

No doubt putting the fear of God into the poor boy. After that talk, I was willing to bet Austin Meadows wouldn't try to so much as hold Madison's hand.

Or not. Teenage hormones were truly a force of nature.

If only Lucille and Mabel had a father like Judge Beck, I thought as I went back to reading.

The next journal entry, the one on the day of Mabel and Harlen's wedding, started with this:

People I love have made decisions that I cannot understand, choices that hurt my soul. Here I sit, deliriously happy with my beloved H, yet feeling heartsick over what has happened. LS is gone, her soul forever damned, and I wonder if I should have opened my eyes, stomped on the ugly envy in my own heart, and perhaps tried to love her too. Could I have made a difference? Only our Lord knows. It is too late to help LS. All I can do is pray for her soul, and put aside my shock and revulsion to extend my hand in loving friendship to the one person who desperately needs me now.

I see storms on the horizon, and I fear the destruction they will inevitably bring.

The journal entry closed with an extremely detailed and almost clinical recounting of the Stevens-Hansen wedding. Then at the very end, almost as an afterthought, she'd written in an unusually messy hand, the page smudged with blotches that looked like they might have been from tears:

I told all to my beloved H. I have never loved him more than I do tonight.

CHAPTER 14

$\mathcal{I}$ took a moment to make a pot of tea and calm my aching heart. Then I returned to the dining room to put aside the journal and went back to the newspaper archives, noting cynically that the Stevens-Hansen wedding took up far more valuable real estate in the paper than the brief note concerning Lucille's suicide. As Evie had said, she'd been found floating in the Hostenfelder pond by a very young Joshua Hostenfelder who was awake early collecting duck and goose eggs.

Joshua Hostenfelder. The name brought a smile to my lips, and I reached out to caress the journal beside my laptop. Evie and Howard's daughter Sarah was to marry him. They were the grandparents that Suzette spoke of. Imagining little Josh searching for eggs was so at odds with what I'd heard of the grumpy old man who regularly chased neighborhood kids out of his pond. It made me smile.

But the smile faded. The pond. The same pond that still sat behind Suzette's house on the two acres that remained of what had once been a huge farm. The same pond Daisy and her friends had secretly swum in. The pond where Lucille

Stevens had ended her life. No wonder an elderly Josh had chased the local kids away from the pond. Each time he saw them, it must have called up the memory of a beautiful young woman, her skin ashen as she floated in the murky water.

The body had been quickly identified as Lucille Stevens, then taken off to the morgue after the family had been notified. I bookmarked the archived date to come back later and read about the wedding in the society pages, then scrolled ahead to see if there was some mention of where Lucille had been interred.

The notice was so tiny I would have missed it had I not been searching so diligently. I hadn't expected her to be buried in the family plot next to her mother since Lucille's father had kicked her out of the house and disowned her, but I hadn't quite expected what the paper told me. Due to her cause of death, Lucille was unable to be buried in the churchyard at all. She was interred in a pauper's grave in the little non-denominational cemetery at the edge of town where the city put the vagrants.

This was too much heartache to handle for a Thursday night. I went back to read about Mabel's wedding, taking in the extensive guest list, the detailed description of the ten-course reception dinner, the stately orchestral music. It had been formal, elegant, and ostentatious, and the bride had been described as stunningly beautiful, her somber mien attributed to the shadow her sister's suicide had cast over the event. I couldn't imagine having to go through with my wedding the day after my sister had been found dead, but I supposed a huge event like that would have been difficult to postpone. Plus, it was unlikely that either Mabel's father or Harlen would have wanted to hold off the wedding out of respect for a sister who had been kicked out of her home, cut off from her family, and who had committed suicide. But Mabel clearly grieved. Was this what had driven her to haunt the furniture? I looked up at the ghost in the corner, wondering if I had Lucille's remains moved to the church-yard, would her sister finally be at peace? Although I had no idea how I was to do that. Relocating remains would cost thousands that I didn't have, and I wasn't sure the church-yard would be any more open to accepting a suicide now than they were ninety years ago.

If this was Mabel's guilt, there might be nothing I could do to help her. I could direct Matt to Lucille's grave and hope he would occasionally go to pay his respects, but I wasn't sure that would be enough. I wasn't sure anything would be enough. There were some things that went so deep they couldn't be healed. It could be that I'd be stuck with Mabel's ghost as long as I owned the sideboard. And as much as I didn't like the idea of having another ghost in the house, I was reluctant to get rid of the piece of furniture. Not only did I truly love it, but I *knew* this ghost. I couldn't shuffle her off to someone who didn't know her story, who didn't tear up thinking about her sister, who couldn't even see her.

I closed the lid on the laptop and stacked the journals back on the chair, giving Judge Beck a quick smile as I headed into the kitchen. I'd reached the end of my emotional well for the evening. It was time to turn my attention to the living, and start preparations for this weekend's neighbor-hood barbeque.

The lights and decorations sat in a big plastic tub by the back door, ready to be put out tomorrow. There were glass fish bowls and colored cabochons for floating candles, sturdy paper plates and utensils as well as plastic wine glasses. I'd brought up a huge copper tub that I planned on filling with ice and a variety of beers and sodas, and another smaller tub for the bottles of wine.

I had burgers in the fridge along with bratwurst soaking in beer. The Larses were bringing three bean and corn salsa with chips. The Steadmans were bringing a marinated carrot salad. The Wilsons were making strawberry rhubarb muffins. There would be Mexican eggplant, Cajun cabbage, green tomato pie, fried soft shell crabs, and even Bob Simmons' squirrel gumbo. Suzette had told me that she was bringing homemade polenta and figs with prosciutto. Daisy was supplying the wine—of course—along with a special bottle of something-something for later. There would be enough food to feed pretty much everyone in the entire town, but I still felt the urge to contribute something of my own.

Plus, baking soothed me. I hoped someday I'd get the same sense of calm and peace from knitting, but right now that hobby was still somewhat frustrating and sadly involved tearing out just as many rows as I'd knitted some nights. Baking was different. As I combined ingredients, I couldn't help but envision my mother and grandmother doing the same. And as the smells filled the house, I imagined all the generations who'd baked for their friends and families right here in this very kitchen. So, it was with that sense of nostalgia that I pulled out my mother's collection of Pillsbury Bake-Off Cookbooks from the fifties.

When she'd passed away, I'd lovingly brought these into my own home, thrilled with the little surprise hand-typed recipes that I occasionally found nestled between the pages. I might not have had any desire to recreate her salmon loaf or savory meat-and-vegetable gelatins, but nothing sent me back to my childhood like Jim Dandies, and Pitty-Pat Pies.

Madison was in charge of making her father's birthday cake when they came back on Sunday, but I wanted to do something festive, so I pulled out all the books and marked down cakes that I thought would appeal to both Judge Beck and my neighbors. Lemon Tea Cake? Strawberry Alaska? Or a Double Devil's Food?

Madison was leaning toward chocolate, so I decided to do the lemon cake instead, figuring it would be a refreshing finish to the variety of meat and side dishes. The recipe made a nine-inch square cake, so I doubled it to end up with two—hopefully enough for all the neighbors. Pulling out my bowls and pans, I gathered the ingredients together, grating the lemon rind and brewing the strong black tea which served to soak the chopped golden raisins.

Sifting the dry ingredients, I cut the shortening into the sugar and beat in two eggs, then alternated folding in the dry ingredients with the liquid reserved from soaking the raisins. Incorporating the raisins, I turned it all into my greased and floured baking dishes and slid them into the oven. This recipe, as well as many of the other ones I had, including the family red velvet cake one, used baking soda as a rising agent. It gave a less uniform rise to the cake, but I loved the moist airiness that these old recipes had compared to the modern store-bought-in-a-box cakes.

While the cakes were cooking, I made the icing, which was a simple buttercream with egg yolk, lemon juice, and lemon zest. I'd wait to ice the cakes until just before the party, but it felt good to have everything prepared and ready to go.

Soothed by my evening baking, I pulled the cakes out of the oven to cool, secured away from a very interested Taco, then went upstairs with my knitting. I was determined to find out all I could about Lucille, but that would wait for tomorrow. Tonight, I planned on relaxing in bed with my cat and my ghost, and attempt to finish off the blue and white striped baby hat that I'd been working on the past few days. The sad story of Mabel and Lucille Stevens had waited for ninety years to be told. It could certainly wait one more night.

.

CHAPTER 15

The next morning, I headed out a bit early, right after my morning yoga with Daisy. On the way to work, I made a detour to a tiny cemetery at the edge of town.

Actually, Merciful Mother Cemetery was no longer on the edge of town as it had been decades ago. Locust Point had grown up and around the small patch of weeds and rain-pitted headstones, and what had once been rural roads and fields were a WaWa and a townhouse subdivision.

I waved to a caretaker who was busy with a very overdue weed whacking and made my way around the rows of tiny, nearly indecipherable headstones. Many graves only had metal markers, the deceased's family unable to scrounge up enough for a headstone over the years. The cemetery wasn't as large as the one behind St. Peter's, but I quickly realized that small was a relative term. There were hundreds of graves here, not just vagrants and the poor, but those who for various reasons had not been buried in the churchyard or the huge newer cemetery with the mausoleum over by the carnival grounds. Deciding that I needed help if I was to find Lucille's grave and get to work on time, I went back to the man trimming grass and caught his attention.

"I'm so sorry to bother you," I told him. "I'm looking for Lucille Stevens' grave. She died and was buried here in June of 1926."

He grinned, wiping a sweaty hand across his forehead and smearing a line of dirt on his brow. The guy looked in his late sixties. I wondered if he did landscaping for a living and this was a contract job, or if he had loved ones buried here and was trying to keep the place tidy on his own time.

"Oh, that's an easy one. See that big stone there? That's her."

I stared, flabbergasted. "That's Lucille Stevens' marker? Her father threw her out of the house over a scandal. She committed suicide and was buried in a pauper's grave."

He nodded. "My family does groundskeeping here, and I remember Dad telling me when the woman had the stone put in. Always thought it looked weird with all the town-provided metal plaques and the modest stones to have that big thing smack in the middle of it all. Dad said she must have held a whole lot of grief in her heart to spend all that money on a marker for a woman that had been dead nearly twenty years when she had it installed."

I fell in beside the man as we walked to the stone. Mabel. It had to have been Mabel. And twenty years would have put the marker placement at roughly 1946. Harlen Hansen had died in 1945. Either Mabel or her daughter had put the stone in right after Harlen had died, and I was betting it was Mabel.

Had it helped her feelings of guilt? Judging from her pleading for forgiveness, I guessed the answer was 'no'.

"No one visits anymore," the man told me. "I keep all the stones neat and the grass trimmed, although with all the rain it's gotten a bit out of hand lately. I haven't seen anyone visiting this grave since I started caretaking here over thirty years ago."

Mabel passed away in 1980. I wondered if Eleonore had even known about her aunt. Certainly Matt hadn't.

Lucille Stevens – December 18, 1907 – June 1, 1926. Beloved Sister.

It brought tears to my eyes, and I leaned down to rub my hand across the lettering. I didn't have to lean down far because the black granite stone was pretty tall.

Brushing the dirt off the base of the stone, I put the flowers I'd brought down, securing the biodegradable pot with little metal stakes. Once more, I felt the sting of tears in my eyes. Lucille had gone through so much in her short life. Young and free spirited, she'd ended so tragically. And to be buried here…. It seemed like a nice cemetery, but the rest of her family was behind St. Peter's, and here she was, surrounded by strangers, once again the outcast even with the fancy headstone.

Lucille needed visitors. And I needed to talk to Matt and his father. It might be a bit deceptive on my part to continue to lead the man on, but I needed to get Matt and his father here, to reunite them with their family. Maybe then poor Mabel could finally rest in peace.

Before I'd even cracked open one of my files at work, I called Matt to tell him that his Grandmother's sister had died at nineteen and that she was buried in the city cemetery.

I heard Matt suck in a breath in shock. "She was nineteen when she died? Good grief, that's awful. No wonder Grandmother never mentioned her. She must have been devastated."

"It gets worse," I told him. "Your Great -aunt Lucille was kicked out of her home about six months before her death after she was caught in a compromising situation with a married man. She committed suicide the day before your grandmother's wedding."

"Wow." His voice was full of shock. "And you think that this is what Grandmother was talking about, the guilt she carried?"

"I think so."

"I had no idea," Matt said. "And I'm sure Mom didn't, either."

And now came more awkward questions. It was a wonder Matt even answered the phone when I called anymore. "Matt, I have to ask, did your mother, Eleonore, ever mention anything about her father? About the fact that she was born six months after Mabel and Harlen's wedding?"

Matt chuckled. "Oh, we all knew that little secret. Seems Grandpa Harlen was a bit impatient to get started on the consummation part of the marriage, no matter what Dad said about him. And it's not like Mom couldn't figure that one out. Her whole life she'd celebrated her birthday in March. She said when she went to get her passport, there was a problem with her Pennsylvania birth certificate. Mind you, in the forties there was still a big percentage of unregistered births. But Mom *had* a birth certificate, it was just fake. Evidently Grandma had paid to have a forged one done, because when Mom finally got around to ordering a new one from Pennsylvania, it had a different birth date on it than the fake one."

"Did she ever ask her mother?"

"No, are you kidding? Grandma adored my mom, but this was clearly a matter of great embarrassment for her. It wouldn't do anyone any good to have it all brought up. Mom just corrected the information on her license, then started celebrating her birthday in December, and never said a word. Neither did Grandma." Matt laughed. "I'm positive my grandparents weren't the only couple that jumped the gun.

They were engaged. The wedding plans were in the works. I'm sure it seemed silly to wait."

"Then why sneak off out of state to have the baby and buy a forged birth certificate?"

"Grandma was a proud woman with a spotless reputation. And I'm sure Harlen Hansen, notable businessman, didn't want to be known as the guy who couldn't wait to get in his nineteen-year-old fiancée's pants."

I winced. "A man that eager, but Eleonore was his only child? All those years of marriage with a beautiful woman that he desired so much he couldn't wait for the ring to be on her finger, then after the wedding he barely speaks to her and doesn't have any other children?"

Matt hesitated a moment before responding. "What are you saying?"

I'd been wrong. *This* was the moment where he ran screaming and told me to never call him again. The thought made me sad, but I had to know.

"What if your grandmother had been in love with someone else? What if she'd loved someone completely unsuitable, and found herself pregnant?"

"Then she could have married him instead," Matt insisted. "Are you implying that Grandmother was fooling around with someone while she was engaged to Harlen? Because I'm counting the months, and she would have gotten pregnant in March. I'm pretty sure she was engaged at that point."

"Just hear me out. Mabel saw what happened to her sister. Her twin had been thrown out of the house, disgraced and homeless with no money, no way to support herself. Suppose the man she loved was unsuitable, someone her father would never approve of, or that couldn't support her. Or maybe she hadn't even met this man when she'd gotten engaged to Harlen. Either way, she gets engaged to Harlen, and three months into their engagement, she falls in love and gets pregnant. She makes a terrible mistake, and now doesn't know what to do."

"I'm sure Grandmother had her faults, but I can't imagine her deceiving Harlen like that," Matt retorted.

"Women back then didn't have much in the way of career opportunities. Where would she have turned as a young pregnant woman? Her sister was already homeless. Even now young women in that position end up prostitutes. As horrible as it sounds, the only way for her to ensure her child didn't starve, had a safe place to live, was to marry Harlen."

"What, and hope he never figured it out? Why didn't she just run off with her lover?" Matt sighed. "I'll admit the idea of Harlen Hansen getting it on with Grandma before the wedding isn't all that believable from the stories Dad tells about him, but it's hard to think that Grandma could have done such a thing. She wouldn't have deceived a man about whether the child she was carrying was his."

"What would you do to make sure your child was safe? And maybe she *did* tell Harlen. She had to have known that he'd figure it out. Maybe she came straight with him, and that's why he was so cold to both her and your mother."

He made a noise of frustration. "Either Grandma deceived her fiancé after cheating on him, or Harlen married a woman who was pregnant with another man's child. Neither one sounds like the people I knew, or that my father knew. Besides, this is all old history. Grandma is gone. Mom is gone. It doesn't matter anymore whether Harlen was Mom's father or not. You're probably right, given that he didn't even leave any of his money to his wife or Mom, but it doesn't matter now."

I winced. "I'm so sorry. I know I sound like a nosy busy-body dragging all this up and possibly slandering your grandmother and grandfather's memories, but I'm hoping that if I get to the bottom of all this, your grandmother's ghost will leave."

"I'd forgotten about the ghost," Matt admitted. "But I don't see why Mom's biological father would have anything to do with a guilt that was so pervasive it made Grandma stick around, haunting that sideboard for decades. Mom was loved, had a wonderful life, was cheerful and happy. There's no guilt there. And from what I heard about Harlen Hansen, I can't imagine any guilt for how she treated him would have caused Grandma a moment's grief."

"How about your mother's real father?" I asked. "Assuming this is all correct, then your Mom married Harlen and left this other man."

Matt thought for a moment. "No. Grandma never seemed the mercenary type. If Mom wasn't Harlen's, then whoever her real father was, he was either dead or had run off when he found out Mom was pregnant. Otherwise I'm pretty sure Grandma would have broken things off with Harlen and married him instead."

"Maybe I'm wrong," I told him. "I'm hope I'm wrong, but I want to keep digging. It's not just that I'd like your grandmother to stop haunting my dining room furniture, but I'd like her to be at peace. After reading all this stuff about her and her sister, I feel like I owe it to her to find out what happened." I bit my lip, worried that maybe I'd pushed things too far. This was Matt's family, after all. It wasn't my business sticking my nose into all this. Well, it wouldn't have been my business aside from the fact that his grandmother had taken up residence in my dining room.

"Keep digging," he told me. "I think you're off in a wrong direction about Mom and Grandma, but I'm glad you found out about my great-aunt. And I want to know, even if it's a horrible scandal. I still want to know."

That was a relief. "So you're not mad at me? I mean, I wouldn't blame you if you were."

He laughed, and this time the sound was warm and friendly. "No, I'm not mad at you. Let me know if you find anything else out, okay?"

"I will," I promised. Then I did something completely on impulse. "Hey, what are you doing tomorrow night? I'm having a neighborhood barbeque at my house to introduce everyone to my new roommate. Would you like to come?"

There was no hesitation at all in his response. "Yes, I'd love to. What can I bring?"

"Nothing. There will be enough there to feed a third-world country," I teased. I told him the time and gave him my address, oddly pleased that he was going to be there.

"Can't wait. I'll see you then, Kay," he said.

I'd no sooner disconnected with Matt then my phone rang. I answered right away because it was Judge Beck. He'd never called me before. I hadn't even realized he had my number, although I must have given it to him when he first moved in.

"Come meet me for lunch," he said, in lieu of a greeting.

I eyed the stack of files that I hadn't even looked at. I shouldn't. It was Friday and I hated going home to the weekend without having all my work done. But Judge Beck had never asked me to lunch before. He'd never called me before.

"I'll buy," he bribed. "And I've got something that you really want to see."

Now I was irresistibly curious to know what he had to show me. "Say no more. Well, tell me when and where, then say no more because I'll be there."

"Noon at the courthouse. I'll tell them I'm expecting you and they'll escort you to my office."

Oh, wow, I'd never been inside a judge's chambers before,

which sounded kind of naughty now that I thought about it. Although I was sure nothing untoward ever happened in Judge Beck's chambers.

"I'll be there," I told him, hanging up to grab the stack of files. I'd need to hustle and get as much done as I could this morning, because there was no way I was going to be late for this lunch meeting.

CHAPTER 16

$\mathcal{A}$ man in uniform with a pistol in a holster at his hip escorted me to Judge Beck's chambers. I was oddly excited about the whole thing. I'd been at the courthouse several times before to pull records for J.T. or to assist him in meeting bail clients, but this was the first time I'd been behind the scenes.

After a quick knock, my chaperone opened the door and I walked past him. Judge Beck's 'office' wasn't as large or plush as the ones I'd seen on television shows, but it appealed to me the same way my parlor did at home. The walls were lined with dark wooden bookshelves. Each shelf held leather bound, gold embossed, thick reference books, held upright by weighty brass bookends. A walnut coatrack stood in the corner, holding a set of dark robes. The judge sat behind an enormous desk, covered with papers as well as his computer equipment.

He smiled when he saw me, rising to his feet. "Thanks, Eric," he told the guard, or bailiff, or whatever he was.

"No problem, Judge Beck." The man closed the door behind him as he left.

"So, this is where all the magic happens," I teased, going to read the titles on one of the bookshelves.

"Actually, the magic happens in the courtroom. This is where I hide away from the drama and the annoying attorneys."

"Aren't you one of those annoying attorneys?"

"Absolutely, but when you're a judge, it's permissible to be annoying. Expected even." He loosened his tie and came around the edge of the desk, picking up a folder. "I've got autopsy results from Lucille Stevens right here. I was going to just bring them home to you, but I'm far too curious to find out what they say. You've got me completely hooked on this family drama, and I don't think I can wait for tonight to see this. I didn't feel right sneaking a peek without you here, so I'm glad you were free for lunch."

I eyed him in surprise. "You pulled autopsy results from ninety years ago? I had no idea they were even available, let alone something you could find in a few hours. Did you spend the morning in some basement dungeon with the microfiche reader?"

"My paralegal spent the morning in the basement dungeon with the microfiche reader. Judges don't need to stoop to such lowly things as pulling records. Although she didn't do it alone. She enlisted the help of a few people in the Records Department, so it didn't take very long to locate."

And these people in the Records Department all jumped to it, no doubt, wanting to stay on this man's good side.

"It's good to be a judge," I said in the same tone that I would have said "it's good to be king".

"Yes, it is." He put his hand on my back and steered me toward the door. "I'm starving. And there's a deli across the street that makes an amazing Ruben."

Sounded good to me. I let the judge herd me toward the elevators, then through the main courthouse lobby where he nodded and smiled to pretty much everyone we passed. It *was* a bit like being in the presence of royalty.

We crossed the street to a busy deli. I sat, holding a table near the front window while Judge Beck went to order our sandwiches at the counter. Before heading up, he put the folder on the table with strict orders for me not to look at it until he got back.

He was just as excited about this case and interested in these people's lives as I was. This was fun, sharing this adventure with him. Well, it would have been fun had it concerned anything other than a woman who had been desperate enough to end her life. I looked down at the folder, not expecting it to reveal much. My main interest was whether Lucille had been pregnant or not at the time of her suicide. I supposed so since that would have added to her troubles even more. A single woman might have been able to convince friends to let her stay in a spare room, possibly even recommending her for employment. A single pregnant woman wouldn't have had even that opportunity.

Judge Beck returned with a tray, placing one plate and a fountain drink in front of me, and another opposite. He slid into the chair and watched me expectantly.

"Sandwich first, or autopsy results first?" I asked.

"Both." He nodded to the folder. "Go ahead and read it out loud. I swear I didn't peek at it, so I'm eager to hear what it says."

He would be a huge help in interpreting the autopsy report. I'd seen enough CSI shows that I thought I'd be able to muddle through the terms and notations, but the judge had far more direct experience than I had.

"You sure?" I looked around the room. "I don't want to gross anyone out on their lunch hour."

"Pretty much every customer in this deli works at the courthouse. They've heard worse. Heck, they've seen worse with some of the crime scene photos that get shown during murder trials. I doubt there's anything too gory in the report anyway. She drowned."

True. I took a bite of my sandwich before opening the folder, and almost decided to wait on the autopsy report. The corned beef was amazing, and the rye bread tasted like it had been baked in-house.

Curiosity won over hunger, and in between bites I managed to scan down the first page of the report.

"Name. Date of birth. Ethnicity. Height and weight," I read. "Physical description says bluish-gray skin tone. Eyes open—that's creepy. Dark hair wavy and wet about eleven inches at the longest point."

Judge Beck leaned forward, reading upside down. "Cold. Clothing intact but sodden. Dress. Silver chain around her neck. She was missing a shoe."

I grimaced, wondering if that shoe was still at the bottom of the Hostenfelder pond. "Lividity fixed in the distal portions of the limbs. No scars, markings, or sign of any recent injuries. Fingernails are short and beds are blue."

"That rules out her hitting her head on something and accidently drowning," Judge Beck commented. "The coroner would have noted an open and recent head wound if that had been the case."

I nodded and continued. "Internal examination of mouth and throat shows no lesions and no injuries to lips, teeth, or gums. No obstruction of airway. Then there's a whole bunch of medical stuff that I don't understand, then the weight of the lungs and a note that they had water and debris consistent with inhalation of pond or river water."

"Heart normal. Gastrointestinal system normal. Urinary system normal," Judge Beck added.

"Could she swim?" I wondered. "I'd imagine it would be difficult to drown yourself otherwise."

"It's not like she weighed herself down with anything, so I'm assuming she couldn't swim."

I shook my head. It just seemed like it would have been easier for her to down a bunch of opium that seemed to be readily available back then. If Lucille was a party girl who smoked and drank, she probably had friends who could supply her with the stuff. Or possibly not. Friends might not have wanted to give her drugs, especially if they thought she was suicidal. And Lucille had been kicked out without much more than the clothing on her back. It wasn't like she had money to buy anything or had a gun. I still felt like maybe slitting her wrists or jumping off a bridge would have been an easier death than walking into a muddy pond and trying to force yourself to stay underwater long enough to drown.

"It's not like the Hostenfelder pond is that deep," Judge Beck added. "It's pretty shallow except in spring when we have a lot of rain. Henry was pestering me last month to ask Miss Hostenfelder if he could swim in it with his friends, so I asked her."

"And?" Suzette hadn't said anything about Henry swimming in her pond, so I assumed either she or the judge had told the boy 'no'.

"She said her grandfather was always worried about the neighborhood kids drowning in it, and I can see why if he was the one who'd found Lucille's body, but it's maybe six feet deep in the center at most. The edges are really muddy and there's a lot of swampy sections, especially since the dock crumbled. She said she was more worried about the kids stepping on nails from the old dock than drowning. We decided it wasn't a good idea for them to swim there right now. And when you fixed the hot tub, Henry pretty much forgot about it."

A clean hot tub beat a muddy, swampy pond any day in my book, but I wasn't a thirteen-year-old boy.

"Maybe she got really drunk beforehand and just passed out facedown in the water," I guessed.

The judge pulled the autopsy report over toward him and paged through it. "It doesn't say that, but I don't know how thorough autopsies were back in the twenties. They probably didn't have the toxicology that they do now. And with the body in water, she wouldn't smell like alcohol."

"And if she ingested as well as inhaled the water, it might not be easy to tell from the contents of her stomach." I eyed the report, wondering if they did blood tests back then.

"Well, here's what you were looking for." The judge turned the papers around and pointed to one paragraph. "She wasn't pregnant."

No evidence of having previously given birth. Not pregnant at the time of death. All pelvic structures are intact and there was no indication of violation or recent activity. Then the report went on to list a whole bunch of medical mumbo-jumbo that I couldn't understand.

Wait. "It says all pelvic structures are intact. That sounds to me like she was a virgin. What else could that mean?"

Judge Beck shrugged. "I can't imagine anything else, but I can send the M.E. a quick text and ask him. Maybe she *was* a virgin."

"But the police chief saw her. Silas Albright was seated with his pants down, and she was straddling him. If he wasn't…you know, then why would she be in a position like that? It's not like they'd be involved in…other things with her sitting on his naked lap."

This was turning into a rather embarrassing conversation to be having with my roommate. And then it hit me.

"Lucille and Mabel were twins. The police chief saw her from the back, then a brief profile at night in a park. What if it wasn't Lucille that was having an affair with Silas, but Mabel? What if the police chief just assumed it was Lucille, because she was the wild party girl, and he never would have expected shy, almost-engaged Mabel to be having sex with a married man?"

Judge Beck stared at me. "Kay, that would make Mabel a truly horrible person. Not only would she have married Harlen Hansen while she was pregnant with another man's child, but if I'm calculating things correctly, she continued to have an affair with Silas after she was caught, after she'd gotten engaged. And she let her sister take the blame for her indiscretion. She let her sister get kicked out of the house into the streets, wrongfully accused of being the one having sex in the park with Silas. Then she continued to have that affair, got pregnant, and refused to help her sister, leading to her suicide."

"I know." It made me sick to think of it. No fancy tombstone could ever make up for that. If it were true, Mabel could beg for forgiveness all she wanted. As far as I was concerned, she wouldn't receive it.

"Maybe they both were a bit wild, and Evie was just blind to Mabel's actions because they were friends and she hid it better than Lucille. Maybe I'm wrong about the coroner's report, and Lucille *wasn't* a virgin at her death."

The judge's phone beeped and he looked down at the screen. "Or maybe the M.E. back in 1926 was a complete idiot and couldn't tell an intact hymen from a broken one. I'm gonna take this down to our morgue and see if we're missing anything. I just don't want to believe that Mabel was capable of such evil."

Neither did I.

CHAPTER 17

"So," Judge Beck said as he came through the door with the ever-present box of files in his hands. The guy hadn't even set his work down and he was clearly eager to tell me his news.

"So? I take it you went down to the morgue this afternoon and showed Lucille's autopsy to the M.E.?"

"Yes. It seems quite possible that Lucille was a virgin. Whoever did the autopsy was a bit of a prude, and unfortunately didn't spell it out with enough clarity for us to be positive, but it appears that's what he meant when he said that her pelvic area was intact. Phil said that it might be possible that the couple hadn't achieved complete penetration when they were interrupted."

"Or it wasn't her," I added.

"Or it wasn't her." The judge sat down his box. "I still don't want to believe that. It's not just Mabel who let her sister take the blame, but that Silas guy, too."

I didn't want to believe it, either. I could see that maybe Mabel, pregnant and scared, had agreed to marry Harlen and had turned her sister away, but not this. This was just too terrible.

"There's more," the judge told me. "Phil said that from what he's reading in the autopsy report, it should have been listed as a murder, not as a suicide."

I blinked a few times. "What? What are you talking about? She didn't have any wounds. What do you mean murder?"

"Phil said there were some notes of what he'd call defensive wounds around her fingernails where she'd clawed and scratched, and that there was petechial hemorrhaging that indicated she was held under water, strangled, then when the murderer let up, she instinctively inhaled water and drowned."

And now my thoughts were going in a completely different direction. Murdered. Someone murdered Lucille and covered it up to make it look like a suicide. But who would want her dead? Mabel, if she was worried that Lucille would claim it wasn't her with Silas, especially if the sister had something that would prove it was Mabel who'd been in the park with the man. Or the father who might have been enraged enough to kill Lucille if she persisted in hanging around town after he'd kicked her out. Or Silas. Or Silas's wife.

A married man who'd just had news of his affair splashed across the gossip page of the paper. His wife might not believe him if he told her the affair was over, but with Lucille dead…. And if Mabel was his lover, then he could continue on with her and no one would know differently.

Or his wife—a big, burly and strong wife if she managed to drown Lucille—determined to make sure her husband never strayed again.

I pulled out my laptop, deciding that the roast in the oven could stay there a bit longer. Plopping down at the table, I pulled up the newspaper archives and searched for Silas Albright.

There was the damning gossip column about the indiscretion in the park. And there, in March, was an obituary. I stared at it, completely confused at this point as to what had happened ninety years ago. March. Lucille died in June, so Silas was hardly her murderer. And his wife would have little reason to murder Lucille three months after her husband had died. Was it Lucille's sister? Her father? Had she out of desperation turned to prostitution or some other illegal activity that ended in her murder? I glanced up at the ghost hovering in the corner and wished once more that she would tell me.

Maybe it was time to get Olive back. Maybe if I asked Mabel some very pointed questions, she'd let me know what happened and tell me what I needed to do so she could move on and get out of my dining room.

I'd text Daisy later. In the meantime, I pulled up Silas Albright's obituary and nearly fell out of my chair. Right in front of me was a picture of a handsome man. And there was no denying the resemblance between him and the picture of Eleonore from the wedding photo Maurice had shown me.

Lucille might or might not have been a virgin, but it was clear who Eleonore's father had been. And if Mabel had been sleeping with Silas Albright, then she not only deceived Harlen, but she *had* let her sister take the blame for her activities in the park that night.

I glanced over at Evie's journals. How could someone be so blind to their friend's doings? She'd known Mabel was pregnant out of wedlock. Hadn't Mabel told her best friend about Silas? Hadn't she confessed that it had been her that night? Evie must have known. Was she just as horrible a person as Mabel?

Saving the picture of Silas, I continued to read the obituary, my stomach dropping with every line. He had been twenty-five, married and no kids. He'd worked at Edwin's Tool and Dye and had graduated from Milford High. But the obituary wasn't the only mention of Silas Albright in the paper archives. A week before the obituary, an article in the paper told that Silas Albright had been found beaten to death in the very park where he'd been caught with Lucille—or Mabel—Stevens. Robbery. He'd fought back, according to the abrasions on his knuckles. But as hard as I searched, I couldn't find that the police had ever found his murderer.

I got up and went into the kitchen to see Judge Beck. "Hey, do you think that paralegal of yours can check on what might be an unsolved murder from March of 1926? Silas Albright. He was found robbed and beaten to death in Freedom Park."

"Sure. Silas Albright was the married lover of at least one of the Stevens girls, right?"

"Yep. And it looks like it was Mabel because Eleonore looked just like him. He died in March, three months before Lucille did."

Judge Beck looked disgusted at the news. "I thought I liked Mabel, but now I kind of hate her. She has an affair with a married man, lets her sister take the blame for it. Then she gets engaged, keeps on having sex with the married guy on the sly, then marries Harlen before he even realizes she's pregnant. What a horrible woman."

"I know. I keep hoping I'll find something else, something that absolves Mabel of all this, but the deeper I dig, the worse it gets."

"You keep looking," the judge told me. "I'll take care of this roast and make us a salad. I won't be able to check on Silas's murder until Monday when my paralegal is back in the office, and I don't think I can wait that long to find out the rest of this story."

Me too. I spun around and went back to the dining room table, picking up Evie's 1926 journal once again. I'd skipped over the early part of the journal and gone straight to June, reading of Lucille's death, the wedding, then reading on to the pregnancy months.

The date Silas's body was found, Evie noted that Mabel had come over, that she was upset. She didn't reveal why, but at the end of the visit, Mabel told Evie that she was going to marry Harlen Hansen.

Wait. Mabel had gotten engaged to Harlen Hansen in January. Had she broken the engagement? Had she planned to, but with the death of Silas, she'd no longer had a reason to reject Harlen? In March, Mabel wouldn't have known she was pregnant. It would have been too soon.

I looked at the journal, realizing that I couldn't continue to skip around, that I'd need to read the whole thing front to back because clearly in between the endless recipes and minutiae, I was missing important things.

I was up until after midnight, giving Judge Beck quick updates while he finished up dinner, cleaned the dishes, then sat down with his own work. When I finally scooped up Taco and climbed the stairs to bed, I was shaken, and I knew the judge was equally appalled at what my reading had revealed. Mabel Stevens had told Evie that she'd broken off her engagement with Harlen in February after only being engaged a month. She told her friend that she was in love with someone else, and although she'd tried to forget this man and move on, she didn't feel it was fair to marry Harlen when her affections lay elsewhere.

This was never announced in the paper. I could only imagine that both Harlen and Mabel's father thought she'd change her mind. And she had, right after Silas Albright was murdered. Maybe it was a sad coincidence, but I found myself thinking how fortunate for Harlen that his rival, married or not, was taken out of the picture, allowing him to win the hand of Mabel. The joke was on him though, as he'd marry her but he'd end up raising a child that wasn't his—the child of a man I was thinking he might have had murdered.

And there was something else. A few weeks before her wedding, before Lucille's drowning, Mabel had given Evie a sealed envelope with instructions to keep it safe and only open it if she died. I searched the rest of the journals, but could find no envelope in any of them. Had Evie eventually destroyed it? Had Mabel asked for it back years later? I had no idea where that envelope was, but I had a feeling it contained the whole story, the one Mabel's ghost clearly wanted someone to hear.

CHAPTER 18

*D*aisy and I both descended on Suzette right after our sunrise yoga, apple spice coffee cake in hand. I didn't have much time before I needed to begin prepping for the party tonight, but I had to know if Suzette knew anything about this sealed envelope that Mabel had given her great-grandmother.

My neighbor answered the door in her pajamas, hair in a ponytail on top of her head. She let us in the moment she laid eyes on the apple spice cake, and immediately set to work putting on a pot of coffee while I brought her up to speed on what had been in Evie's journals.

"I remember my grandfather saying when he was a kid, he'd found someone who'd drowned in the pond," she told us, setting mugs and plates on the table.

"Was that why he never wanted any of us to swim there?" Daisy asked.

"Probably not," Suzette told us. "He told me he was sure the woman had been murdered, that the pond wasn't more than five feet deep that summer because they'd had a dry spell. And he was certain he'd heard people out there late the night before. His bedroom was up in the loft and it gets hot as blazes up there. He said he had the window open and could hear people arguing, then splashing, then in the morning when he went out to look for duck eggs, he saw the body."

"Weren't you like seven or something when he died?" Daisy asked. "That's a pretty harsh story for your grandfather to be telling a young child."

"It was a pretty harsh thing for a young child to find a dead body in the pond," Suzette countered. "We were working on fixing up the dock together one day and I found a nest of duck eggs. I guess it reminded him and he told me the story then. He was a great one for stories. Like the one about when he won the pie-eating contest at the fair to impress my grandmother, only to throw up right in front of her ten minutes later."

Daisy snorted. "Men. Only a guy would think a woman would be impressed by how much food he could cram into his stomach in a short amount of time."

"Feats of competitive gastronomy have always done it for me," I told Daisy in my best deadpan.

"Personally, I'm fond of a partner who isn't afraid to put down a pie or two." Suzette eyed the food on the table. "Or apple crumb cake. Or that gingerbread you brought by the other day. I'm a girl who isn't ashamed of enjoying quality baking."

Daisy raised her hands. "Okay, I'm clearly outnumbered here by you gluttons. Did your grandfather do anything else notable in his life beyond speed-eating pie and finding murder victims?"

Suzette brought over the coffee pot and poured us all a mug, then sat down to slice into the cake. "Let's see...he was quite skilled at marbles when he was young. I still have jars with the ones he won. And he knew how to butcher a hog, although he told me his parents got rid of all the pigs when they sold off the majority of the land here. Oh, and he had a lovely tenor singing voice. Gran always said that was the reason she married him."

"Not because of his pie-eating skills?" I teased.

She smiled as she put a generous slice of cake on each plate. "I remember him singing me to sleep, and some nights, after I was in bed, I'd hear him singing to Gran. He did have a lovely voice. Wish I had inherited that. All I seem to have as far as my grandfather's skills is the pie-eating one."

"It's a good skill to have." I took a few bites of the cake, which had turned out quite well, if I did say so myself. I only hoped the lemon cake for the party tonight was just as good.

"Actually, I wanted to ask you something about your great-grandmother," I said to Suzette after we'd each moved on to a second piece of cake. "She said in one of her journals that Mabel had given her a sealed envelope back in 1926 before Mabel's wedding to Harlen Hansen, and told your great-grandmother to open it if she died. I wondered if you had come across it at all?"

Suzette paused mid-bite. "An envelope? I didn't find anything in the house when I went through it after my grand-mother's death. But great-grandmother Evie died in 1945, long before her friend Mabel had. If she wasn't supposed to open the envelope unless Mabel died, then she wouldn't have done so. Not like me. I don't think I would have had the self-discipline not to steam it open and take a peek."

"Oh, I would have read it too," Daisy chimed in.

And so would I. Maybe. It would have been a struggle, because if Daisy had given me an envelope like that, my curiosity and desire to know if I could help my friend or not would have warred with the idea that anything she'd wanted me to know, she would have told me.

I'd like to think I wouldn't have opened it, that I would have trusted my friend and quite possibly been scared that the contents might reveal something that could forever change the way I saw her. Some things were better off left unknown.

"What happened to your great-grandmother Evie's things when she passed away?" I asked.

"I wasn't born then, but I do know Sarah, her daughter and my grandmother, had a box of her things. It had the journals, and some jewelry that Evie's husband had given her throughout the years. A few pictures. A braid of hair."

A braid of hair. I remembered Evie pestering her mother to have her long hair cut fashionably short and imagined she'd saved it as some sort of memorabilia.

"Mabel was still alive at the time of your great-grandmother's death. I'm assuming she came to the funeral. And since your grandmother Sarah and Mabel's daughter Eleonore were very close, Sarah might have returned an envelope that was obviously written by Mabel?"

"Probably," Suzette said. "If it was clear on the face of the envelope that it was written by Mabel and that it was private, she wouldn't have read it. Great-granddad Howard lived until 1967, but he most likely would have had his daughter assist in going through Evie's personal things. And if the letter was in the journals, there's a good chance it wasn't even found until years after Evie's death. Or ever found at all."

"I searched all the journals and it wasn't in there," I told Suzette. "I can't imagine that Evie would have kept it elsewhere since it clearly held very personal information. Do you think Mabel would have asked for it back after Evie's death? Or even after Harlen's death?"

Harlen had died just months before Evie had. If I was

right and Harlen had murdered Silas, then Mabel would no longer have needed to fear him.

And yes, it chilled me to think that Mabel had married and had slept with a man who most likely had murdered her lover.

"It's definitely a possibility. They were very close friends. Their daughters were very close friends. Howard would probably not have thought twice about letting Mabel take an envelope back that held a letter she'd written his wife years ago."

Normally I would have thought that Mabel would have proceeded to destroy such a letter. Harlen was dead. There was no need for her daughter to find out about her illegitimacy, or to know that the man she'd considered a father had most likely been a murderer. But if she'd destroyed the letter, wanted all of that to fade away into the past, then why haunt a piece of furniture, a family heirloom, for decades following her death?

We switched the conversation to more pleasant topics, discussing Suzette's continued work on the old farmhouse, whether Harry Peter's nephew planned to sell his uncle's house after he'd finished going through everything or move in himself, who might win this year's regatta, and whether Bob Simmons would add to the dozens of giant holiday inflatables that filled his lawn every year from Thanksgiving until the day after New Years'.

I left the scant remains of the apple crumb cake with Suzette, telling her that I'd see her later tonight at the barbeque, then taking my leave of Daisy as we passed her house. I noticed that Judge Beck's car wasn't in the driveway as I headed up the stairs to my front door. He'd had a golf outing this morning, so he'd need to wait to hear what little information I'd gotten from Suzette. Her grandfather had confirmed that Lucille had been murdered, and not committed suicide. And we were no closer to finding the letter Mabel had written than we were last night.

Had she destroyed it? I was sure if it had been among her effects when she'd passed away, then her daughter would have read it, and Matt would have known all about Eleonore's real father as well as what I suspected about what happened to Silas Albright.

Where was the envelope? I'd pretty much exhausted every research avenue open to me. If the envelope was gone, if it had been inadvertently destroyed, then the secrets died with Mabel. And I wasn't sure even Olive could get the ghost to tell us what she'd had bottled up all those decades.

CHAPTER 19

*J*udge Beck was nearly late to his own party. Daisy and the Larses had already arrived and were helping me cart out food and set up chairs when he came through the back gate, a bag of golf clubs over his shoulder and a folder in his hand.

"I was beginning to wonder if your golf game had gone into overtime," I teased as he leaned the clubs up against the side of the house.

"I ran by the courthouse and actually braved the dungeon records room just to see what I could dig up on the Albright murder," he said, handing me the folder.

There was one sheet of paper in the folder—a copy of a faded form.

"What is this?" I'd hoped he would discover who had been charged for Silas Albright's murder, and if that person had any sort of connection to Harlen Hansen, but this didn't look like a police report.

"It's a preliminary filing for divorce proceedings," he announced. "In February of 1926, Silas Albright filed this paper, and there are several others showing he was continuing to go through with the divorce until his death in March. I wanted to get you copies of those, but the microfiche printer jammed and my law degree didn't give me the appropriate skills to fix office equipment. I'll ask Deanna to get me copies on Monday."

As tragic as this whole story was, I felt a wave of relief wash over me. Mabel had broken up with Silas, gotten engaged to Harlen and tried to make that work, but she was in love. In February, she broke off her engagement to Harlen, and Silas filed for divorce. If he hadn't been killed, Mabel would no doubt have married him and although Eleonore would have probably been born before the ink was dry on their marriage license, they would have been together.

But Silas had been killed in a park, supposedly during a robbery, and a broken-hearted Mabel thought she might as well marry Harlen. It still didn't absolve her of potentially trying to pass another man's child off as Harlen's, or letting her sister take the blame for her indiscretion with Silas, but at least she hadn't been cheating on her fiancé.

And I suspected a jealous Harlen had killed his rival. I could have been wrong. People were murdered in robberies, and there was no saying that Silas's wife might not have had some pretty angry relatives who might have decided to make Silas pay for leaving her, but Harlen was definitely a suspect.

And if he killed Silas, could he have also killed Lucille? Although why? With Silas gone, there was no reason for anyone to want Lucille dead. Except maybe Mabel, and I refused to think that of her. I winced at the thought that both Harlen and Mabel could be murderers. Evie might have worn rose-colored glasses when it came to her friend, but I doubted any sort of cheerful optimism would have disguised the character traits Mabel would need to have to have been a murderer.

Unfortunately, I was at a dead end as far as this investigation went. And I had a party with guests arriving in less than a half an hour. Shooing Judge Beck and his golf clubs into the house, I tucked the folder into my briefcase and pulled my lemon cakes out of the fridge to ice.

The party was in full swing when Matt finally arrived. All the neighbors had come, as well as J. T., and my friends Carson and Maggie. Even Olive had come, bringing her homemade sangria to share. We'd all taken turns at the grill, and Judge Beck was happily in conversation with Suzette when I saw Matt, a long plastic container in his hand.

"I know you said not to bring anything, but I felt weird coming here empty-handed," Matt confessed, extending a tray of deviled eggs.

"Yum." I sat them down on a table and promptly popped one in my mouth. They were delicious, creamy with a tang that came from the addition of spicy mustard and a liberal sprinkling of Old Bay Seasoning on top. "Let me introduce you around, but first—beer or wine?"

"Beer, please."

I led him over to the copper tub and he eyed the selection, picking one out and popping the cap off. We made the rounds, and I was surprised that a few of the neighbors knew Matt from the VFW's turkey pot pie dinners. I was just getting ready to leave him in Daisy's capable hands and refill the ice when Judge Beck made his way over to us.

"Matt, this is my roommate. Judge Nathanial Beck," I said by way of introductions.

"Nate," the judge said as he extended his hand. "You must be Matt Poffenberger? Kay mentioned you were coming."

"Your roommate?" Matt seemed to have some trouble wrapping his head around that one. I knew I told him that the barbeque was to introduce my new roommate to the neighborhood. Maybe he'd just assumed I'd meant a female roomie?

"For a couple of years until he buys his own place," I told Matt, unwilling to go into personal details about the judge's divorce and custody battle.

"Counting the days already, Kay," Judge Beck teased. "It's my taking over your dining room table for a workspace, isn't it?"

I rolled my eyes. "Yes, because I host so many formal dinners in there. No, I'm not counting the days. I just figured you'd be thinking about a place of your own as soon as things are settled."

He turned to Matt with a knowing grin. "Maybe I better start looking. Where's Carson? I'll have to ask him to keep an eye out for listings. A few years will be here before I know it."

It would. And my house would be horribly lonely without Judge Beck and his kids to keep me company.

"There's a new development going up on the east side of Milford next year," Matt suggested. "Golf course community. You golf, right?"

"Yes, I do." Judge Beck looked around the yard with a fond smile, then turned that fond smile on me. "Although I really love it here. I might just wait until something on this street comes up for sale. You wouldn't mind having me around for a bit longer, would you, Kay? I promise to share the dining room table with you."

"Stay as long as you like," I told him. Two years. Five years. A few decades. As long as he liked.

"I think the golf course subdivision would suit you better," Matt said.

"Maybe, but I'd love it if you bought something here," I said, then turned to Matt. "I've grown very fond of the judge's children. It would be wonderful if they stayed in the neighborhood."

"They're very fond of you too, Kay," Judge Beck added.

"Do you golf, Matt?" I asked, wondering if I needed to

drag my old clubs out of the attic and blow the dust off of them.

"I haven't in years, but I do coordinate the tournament fund raiser at Oak Grove Links. It's one of the major money makers for the children's cancer wing at Milford General."

"I play in that tournament every year," Judge Beck chimed in. "A group of us at the courthouse sponsored a hole last year, too."

"Would you be willing to help me with the fundraiser this year, Kay?" Matt asked, angling his body toward me. "We're always looking for people to help call businesses to see if they'd sponsor a hole, and try to drum up some additional donated prizes."

I'd been wanting to find something to keep me busy, something worthwhile that would take my mind off of Eli and get me more involved in the community, allow me to ease back into a more social existence. This would be perfect.

"I'd love to." Already my mind was whirring with possible prize ideas and places to hit up for donations. "Now, if you'll both excuse me, I'm off to grab another bag of ice from the kitchen freezer, then mingle."

I left the pair of them chatting about golf and refilled the ice buckets, taking a turn at the grill, then discussing knitting and crochet with Suzette and Kat. All too soon, people began to drift home, leaving me with far too many leftovers and alcoholic beverages. When I waved the last guest goodbye, I returned to the backyard to find Judge Beck wiping down the tables.

"Thank you," he told me with a smile. "It feels like it's been forever since I actually went to a party."

"Bob Simmons didn't bore you too much with his 'history of Locust Point' speech, did he?" I asked, grabbing the last few bottles of wine.

"Not at all. And your friend, Matt, is very nice. He's going to join us golfing next week."

This golfing thing was making me feel a bit left out. Maybe I did need to find my clubs as well as take some much-needed lessons. Or I could let the guys have their fun while Daisy, Kat, Suzette, and I all sat on the porch and knitted and drank wine.

"I'm glad you guys hit it off." I handed him a bottle of wine and looped my arm in his. "Leave the rest of this and I'll clean it up later. You've got a busy day tomorrow, birthday boy."

Madison and Henry were to come back here for the week, and the kids had a special meal planned. We walked inside and before I went up to bed, I paused by the dining room, where the ghost still stood. My life was so happy. I'd married the man I loved, and even though I'd lost him too young, I still had friends and family. Even with the grief, there were still moments of sunshine in my life, moments when I felt so happy that I thought my heart would burst.

Mabel had lost so much. And when I thought of her and what she'd gone through, I realized how blessed my life truly was.

CHAPTER 20

*H*eather brought the kids over promptly after church on Sunday. They raced through the door, setting their backpacks and bags aside then throwing themselves into their father's arms with a chorus of "happy birthdays". Heather stood awkwardly to the side, conveying information about a party Henry had been invited to, then went to leave.

She stopped, her hand on the door, and turned back. "Nate? Happy Birthday."

He looked up, his eyes cool, his face expressionless. "Thanks."

With that short word, he pivoted, gathering the kids in his arms once more. Heather eyed them sadly, told Madison and Henry she'd see them next week, then left. My heart ached for her. I knew she was the one who wanted the divorce, but this was obviously hurting her as much as it was Judge Beck. And although I knew he hoped they'd eventually be able to have civil discourse with each other, he still wasn't ready to forgive and forget.

But this wasn't the time to dwell on broken marriages. We had a birthday to celebrate, and Madison had a cake to bake.

The kids couldn't wait to give their father their gifts, and with a stampede of footsteps, they raced upstairs and then back down again, each one clutching brightly wrapped presents.

"This one is from both of us," Madison announced, plopping a gift in her father's lap.

I sat down to watch, curious what they'd gotten him. Heather had taken the kids out to shop for gifts a few weeks ago, earning her some serious bonus points in my book. It couldn't have been easy to fund Madison and Henry's presents to the man who was soon to be her ex-husband.

Judge Beck tore the wrapping paper off and opened up a box, pulling out a mug that had "I love you, Dad" written on it on either side in each of the kids' handwriting. Madison had even encircled her words with a red heart.

"Thank you. I love it." And from the husky note in his voice, I could tell he truly did. I envisioned him drinking his morning coffee from this mug, proudly displaying it in his chambers or even in the courtroom. Were judges allowed to have coffee in the courtroom?

"Look inside." Henry bounced up and down, pointing to the mug. The judge pulled out a piece of paper and read that he'd been given a membership to a coffee-of-the-month club.

Ooooh. I hoped that membership included enough coffee for me to sample as well.

"This one is from both of us, too," Henry said, handing his father a smaller package.

It held a hand-written gift certificate for ten car washes, provided by Madison and Henry, as well as another certificate for a "special breakfast-in-bed."

After another round of hugging, Madison informed her father that he was banned from the kitchen, then turned to me with a smile. "Did you get the ingredients, Miss Kay?"

"I sure did." I'd not only gotten the supplies for the cake, but had also picked up steaks and sweet potatoes for Henry to grill, with supervision, for his father's birthday dinner.

Henry shooed his father out into the back yard with a book and a beer while Madison pulled all the ingredients for her cake out of the cabinets.

She'd selected a classic devil's food cake with fudge icing. When I went in, she had everything neatly lined up on the counter and ready to go—unsweetened cocoa, cake flour, baking soda, butter, superfine sugar, brown sugar, eggs, and vanilla extract. For our first step, I had her cut rounds of wax paper for the bottoms of the cake pans, then butter the pans. Measuring the cocoa into a bowl, she whisked in hot water until it was smooth, then blended in cold water and set it aside as she sifted together her dry ingredients.

"Now cream the butter," I told her as I got the mixer out. Once it was smooth and light in color, she slowly added the white sugar, then the brown sugar, both one tablespoon at a time.

Then we added the eggs and vanilla, alternating the dry ingredients with the cocoa liquid as the final step. Once the cakes were in the oven, we turned our attention to the custard filling and the icing.

Custard is tricky and I'd wanted Madison to skip this part of the recipe, instead using additional icing between the cake layers, but she'd insisted, so I got out the double boiler and set her to whisking the milk, cream, and chocolate while I prepared the sugar, cornstarch, flour and salt. Then I showed her how to quickly whisk the dry ingredients in, stirring constantly to ensure there were no lumps. Once the filling was the consistency of pudding, I showed her how to temper the yolks so we didn't end up with scrambled eggs in our custard, then add the mixture back into the filling. When it was done, we added the vanilla, then let the filling cool on the counter before popping it into the refrigerator.

It was time to get dinner going, so I left Madison to make the fudge frosting and went out to find the judge relaxing in a chair, a fond smile on his face as he watched his son work on the entertainment console and chatted about a video game. I fired up the grill and gave Henry instructions on preparing the sweet potatoes and the seasoned steaks.

While the cakes were cooling and the frosting was chilling with the filling in the fridge, we ate our dinner, then while Madison iced the cake, the judge, Henry, and I played a few hands of Go-Fish.

"Cake time!" Madison brought in her masterpiece and I felt my heart swell with pride. This had been a challenging recipe, and she'd done it with very little direction from me. In addition, she'd assembled and iced the cake completely on her own.

"That looks amazing," Judge Beck said. I'd told him how involved this recipe was, and I knew that he appreciated the effort that had gone into such a creation.

"Let's use the nice china," Henry said, scooting back his chair and pulling plates from the cabinet.

"And the good silver," Madison added. She went over to the sideboard, shivering as she walked through the ghost that was now ever present by the piece of furniture. As she pulled the drawer open, it stuck slightly, and she yanked. It slid free, silverware flying out and the drawer dropping from her hand to the floor where it landed with a crack.

"Miss Kay, I'm so sorry!" Tears glistened in the girl's eyes. "I broke it. It's broken."

I picked up a section of the drawer. "It's not too bad," I assured her, even though my heart had sunk as I saw the two pieces. "Nothing a little wood glue won't fix. See how the sides are joined with this tongue-in-groove fitting instead of nails? We'll just glue it back, attach the bottom, and it will be as good as new."

A tear rolled down Madison's cheek and she sniffed. "It stuck, and I just pulled too hard. I'm so sorry, Miss Kay."

"It was an accident, Madison. I'm not mad, truly I'm not. I'll pick this all up and fix it later, because right now I want some of that cake. We'll just use the kitchen silverware instead."

Both she and Henry darted off to the kitchen and I turned from the broken drawer, trying hard not to cry.

"Is it bad, Kay?" Judge Beck grimaced. "I can look up a professional cabinet maker and pay to have it repaired."

"I'll look at it later." I forced a smile. "Right now, let's just enjoy Madison's cake."

And enjoy it we did, each of us having a huge slice and practically licking our plates clean. Madison was glowing from our praise, and I was pretty sure that Daisy and I were going to be having cake for our post-yoga breakfast tomorrow because it was really that good. When we were done, Madison and Henry went into the kitchen to do the dishes while Judge Beck and I surveyed the broken drawer.

I picked up the two sides while Judge Beck picked up the silverware from the floor. It looked like they could be glued back together, but there were some broken parts.

"Let me find a cabinet maker," he insisted. "It's a beautiful piece of furniture, and I want to make sure it's repaired with quality workmanship. Just put the pieces in a box, and I'll take it to someone tomorrow."

He was right. It really should be repaired by someone

who would do a better job than me with some wood glue and rubber bands. I thanked him and gathered up the pieces while he took the silverware into the kitchen to wash. And that was when I saw it. Taped to the bottom of the broken drawer was an envelope.

A chill ran across my shoulders. I glanced up to see the shadowy spirit off to my side, what looked like an indistinct hand on the top of the sideboard. An envelope. *The* envelope. It was yellow and brittle. Across the front in a thin swirling hand, it said "Open only upon my death—Mabel Stevens".

She must have retrieved it from Evie upon her husband's —or Evie's—death and hidden it in the sideboard. I was such an idiot. Mabel hadn't been haunting the sideboard because it was a family heirloom, she'd been trying to tell us to look inside. Or yank one of the drawers out and look underneath it. My fingers itched to open it, but I wanted to read this in private. And I wanted to share it with Judge Beck.

I walked into the kitchen with the envelope in my hands and showed it to the judge.

"Is that….? Where did you find it?"

"Taped to the bottom of that broken drawer from the sideboard," I told him. He tried to snatch it from my hands and I shoved it behind my back. "Uh-uh. Wait until the kids are in bed, then we'll read it together."

His eyes danced with excitement. "Time to go to bed, kids."

They both shrieked in dismay. It took three more rounds of Old Maid and some hot cocoa before Madison and Henry finally headed up. While the judge was upstairs with the kids, I yanked a bottle of champagne out of the fridge and popped the cork, bringing it, two glasses, and the envelope into the parlor. Plopping down on the sofa, I poured the bubbly. I was pretty sure the contents of this letter were going to be heart-breaking, but it wasn't the sad story I was celebrating, it was that we were finally going to find out what had happened. We'd finally discover the secret Mabel had kept for all these years. And hopefully, now that her letter had been found, Mabel would be able to find peace and forgiveness in eternal rest.

CHAPTER 21

I heard Judge Beck's footsteps on the stairs and handed him a glass of champagne as he sat on the sofa beside me.

"Happy birthday." I raised my glass in a toast.

He returned the gesture. "Yes, yes. Now hurry up and read the letter. I'm dying to know the truth about what happened with Mabel and Lucille."

I took a sip and sat the glass down, sliding my finger under the flap of the envelope and easing out the thin sheets of paper.

March 10, 1926

Dearest Evie,

I know you think me a pure and beautiful person, but I fear that is not the truth. There are things I have kept from you because your love and friendship is something I could not bear to lose. If you are reading this, then it is because I am dead, and I must risk losing your respect to bring the truth to light.

Last year, I met a man and fell in love. I tried to forget him. I tried to stay away because he is married and to be the cause of a man's breaking his marriage vows would be a terrible sin. I tried, but the flesh is weak, and I gave in to sin. It was me, not my sister who was caught in the arms of Silas Albright that night. I immediately returned home and confided in Lucille, who knew that she would be blamed instead of me. I was ready to confess all to Father and bear the brunt of his anger and punishment, but Lucille volunteered to do so in my stead. She has always been the stronger, the more independent twin, and she had plans to run away from home anyway. She had friends who would help her, and a beau that she intended to marry as well as an offer of employment—none of which Father would have ever allowed, as these friends and this beau, were all what he would consider low-class individuals. Because she intended to leave, and knew her actions would lead to being disowned, she offered to take the blame for being seen with Silas.

The incident made me vow never to see Silas again. I am not strong and independent like Lucille, and I do not have a way to support myself or friends who would take me in if it had been brought to light that I had been having an affair with a married man. I know you are thinking that you would have helped me, but you have family of your own to think of, and I would never have jeopardized your future with Howard by putting you in a position where you needed to choose between your spotless reputation and helping a friend.

I broke off all contact with Silas and became engaged to Harlen Hansen. He has been my most devoted and attentive suitor this year, and I felt that with him I could have a satisfying future. Within a month of our engagement, I discovered that there is a side to Harlen that disturbs me. He is jealous and possessive. He can be unkind and vengeful. As I confided in you, I broke off our engagement, but he would not accept that and neither would Father. Both were convinced that I was merely suffering from nervous anticipation, and they proceeded with plans for our wedding in spite of my protests.

A few weeks after I'd broken my engagement, I came upon Silas *while out shopping. We spoke, and he confessed that he still loved me as much as I loved him. He told me that he had filed for divorce from his wife, and that he had secret hopes that I would elope with him once the divorce was final. Oh Evie, I am a weak woman. I fell into his arms, and we resumed intimate relations once more. Last night I very firmly repeated to Harlen that our engagement was indeed off, and that I would not marry him in June, or any other time.*

He knew there was another man, and he told me that he had known it was me with Silas Albright that night and not my sister Lucille. He said he had overlooked it as a youthful indiscretion. He painted a bleak tale of what my life would be like with Silas, of how my father would disown me, how everyone in the town would shun me. He said that Silas would most likely lose his job, and that we would need to move elsewhere. The stain of his divorce and infidelity, of the part I'd played in it, would follow us everywhere. We would live our lives on the edge of poverty, in filth and squalor.

I listened, and I heard the truth in his words. I am not strong like Lucille. It would be difficult to live such a life, and the judgment and scorn of others would cut me deeply. Harlen promised me that he would marry me anyway, that he would forgive me what I'd done in the past with Silas as long as I broke off for good with him. He promised me a life of ease and luxury, a life where no one would look at me in scorn. He said he did not need my love to be happy, only my hand in marriage and my vow to be true to him.

I wavered in my resolve, and asked him to wait for my decision. Today, I have read in the papers that Silas is dead, beaten and robbed in the very park where we shared our love for each other. I might be a foolish young woman, but I cannot help but wonder if Harlen had a part in this.

I hope I am wrong.

Yours truly, Mabel

"There's more," I told Judge Beck, turning to the next sheet of paper.

May 19, 1926

Dearest Evie,

I had been uncertain whether to give you the previous letter or not, as in the harsh light of day, my fanciful accusations of Harlen seemed farfetched. But as our wedding date draws nearer, I wonder once more if he orchestrated the murder of my Silas. My friend, I hate to burden you with this. It brings me great joy to see you and Howard together, to witness your love for each other. I am thrilled that you are expecting a child. Once again, I must remind you that I am not the pure woman you would think me to be as I too am expecting a child of my own.

I was uncertain for a while because monthly events for me are not always predictable and I am often overdue. A few weeks ago, I became convinced of my condition and spoke with Lucille. We meet often, in secret as both Father and Harlen would not approve. She urged me to not go through with the wedding, to come to her and that she would help me.

Evie, I am so weak. I am afraid I could not live as Lucille so happily does. I am afraid that as an unwed mother, I will need to spend my life living on the charity of others, in squalor and poverty. It isn't just me that I fear for, but this child I carry. How could I subject a baby to that sort of life? But the alternative is to marry Harlen and deceive him that this child I carry is his. I have been a sinful woman, but that is a sin I cannot commit. Tonight, I plan to tell Harlen that I carry Silas's child, and that I will not marry him. I know he will worry, for I think he truly loves me, and I know he will be angry, but I will leave him and go to Lucille and pray that God takes pity on an innocent baby born of sin and gives me the means to keep this child healthy and safe.

If I never see you again, I wish you, Howard, and your child the best. You are my dearest, most loved friend, and I cherish the times we have shared. If I die, whether by natural means or otherwise, please look to Harlen, for as much as he says he loves me, I worry that if he cannot have me, he will orchestrate events so that no one else in this world can, either.

Yours truly, Mabel

I took a big drink of my champagne, holding out the glass for Judge Beck to refill. "There's a third letter," I told him. "And I think this one is going to be the hardest to read of them all."

He topped off his own glass. "I feel so bad for this woman, but at the same time, I'm relieved she isn't the horrible person I'd feared. Her sister had volunteered to take the blame for getting caught with Silas. She'd broken off her engagement with Harlen before she'd taken back up with her lover. And it seems she'd told him about the baby and given him the option of ending their engagement."

It was still tragic that Mabel was pregnant, her lover dead, forced to choose between marriage to a man she didn't love and who she suspected had killed the father of her child, and excruciating poverty. Taking a deep breath, I sat down my glass, and began to read the final letter.

June 20, 1946

Dearest Eleonore, beloved child of mine and Silas's heart,

I retrieved these letters after Evie's death and nearly burned them, but I felt there were things you should know.

So many years have passed, and I still feel the weight of guilt. If only I had been stronger. If only I had trusted my intuition more. Two days before our wedding, I told Harlen about you and about my plan to leave and live with Lucille.

The next day Lucille was found dead in the Hostenfelder pond by their little boy. They claim it was a suicide, but I know better. I had just spoken with Lucille and she was as happy and sassy as always. She was murdered, and I am to blame.

I had planned to leave Harlen for Silas, and Silas was murdered. I had planned to leave Harlen and stay with Lucille, and now my sister has been murdered. It became clear to me on that day that Harlen would kill anyone who gave me an avenue to escape him. It also became clear to me that if I continued to refuse to marry him, he would most likely kill me as well.

You are my life. You are all I have left of Silas, and as I sat in my room the morning of my wedding, I realized that I had nowhere to turn. I could not risk my friend Evie's life by asking her and her husband to shelter me, and I could not risk that Harlen would kill me, and thus also kill you, if I refused to marry him. For once in my life, I needed to be strong.

So, I went to Harlen and I told him that I would marry him. I told him that I would remain faithful to him and not break our marriage vows until death we parted. My only condition was that he raise you as his own child, that he never voice the accusation that you were not his own. He agreed, arranging for me to leave the state during my pregnancy to hide that you were older than you should have been. He also arranged for the falsified birth certificate.

He murdered your father. He murdered your aunt. But I made sure he never laid a hand on you. I may have been a weak woman, but the moment you were born, I had to become strong for you.

Eleonore, I love you so, and I am happy you have found love in a good man like Maurice and have a brave and kind son. Matthew reminds me of Lucille in so many ways.

May God have mercy upon my soul. I'm to blame for two murders and I will never forgive myself.

I love you with all my heart, Mother.

Tears were blurring the pages as I sat them down on the coffee table.

"Oh, Mabel," Judge Beck said, his voice husky. "You are not to blame for two murders. Harlen Hansen is to blame, and if this had come before me in my courtroom, I would have sent him to jail. You were honest and truthful to him, and he treated you like you were a possession to own, murdering those who stood in the way of his having you. I'm sorry you spent your life with that man. I'm sorry you lost Silas and Lucille and had to endure being married to a murderer just so your daughter was raised in comfort."

A chill blasted through the room, and I saw her—the ghost of Mabel Stevens. Her shadowy form came into the parlor, for the first time leaving the sideboard and the dining room. Then right before my eyes, she transformed into that nineteen-year-old beauty in the silk dress with her sleek dark hair and cupid's-bow mouth.

"Thank you," she whispered to Judge Beck. Then she smiled and faded away, the chill leaving the room with her smoky outline.

"Did you...did you see that?" I asked the judge, unable to believe that he could possibly have missed the woman who'd stood before him, as clear and as solid as she'd been in real life.

He turned to me with a puzzled frown. "See what?"

CHAPTER 22

I stood by Lucille's grave marker and watched as Matt walked through the uneven ground of the cemetery. Mabel's ghost hadn't returned. It seemed that having her letters found allowed her to finally rest in peace, but I wouldn't feel the story had ended on her life until her grandson saw those letters and read them.

"Odd place for a date," he commented with a smile when he reached me.

"No dates," I told him, deciding I needed to be totally clear about the nature of our non-relationship. "Friends don't have dates, we just get together and drink coffee or do yoga, or work on charity fund raisers."

"And evidently friends hang out in cemeteries," he teased. "I take it you've asked me here to introduce me to my great-aunt Lucille?"

I extended the envelope. "Yes, and to give you this. It was taped to the bottom of a drawer in the sideboard. These were written by your grandmother, Mabel."

He took them and read the three letters in silence. I knew

when he got to the last letter, the one addressed to his mother, because he had to brush a hand across his eyes.

"I wish we had known earlier," he said, folding the letters and carefully putting them in his pocket. "I wish she had told us while she was still alive, then we could have let her know that there was nothing to forgive. How could she have felt such guilt over this? She wasn't the one who murdered Silas and Lucille. She'd never deceived Harlen. And she loved my mother—loved her enough to marry a man who was most likely a murderer just to make sure she wasn't a bastard child starving on the streets. What is there to feel guilty about?"

I'd expressed the same things to Daisy this morning during our yoga, and my friend had opened my eyes to how young girls often feel when they're trapped into making the best of many bad decisions, how they often blame themselves and second guess what they did or didn't do.

"Because she was honest and never deceived Harlen, two people died," I told Matt. "If she had snuck out in the middle of the night and run away with Silas, the scandal would have hit before Harlen had a chance to do anything, and it's possible Silas wouldn't have died. And if she'd just run off with Lucille, been a no-show at her wedding, then her sister wouldn't have died. Because she told Harlen that she was leaving him, she felt to blame for Silas and Lucille's deaths."

Matt nodded. "And even though she did everything in her power to make sure my mother had a wonderful life, I'm sure for an honest person like my grandmother, the deception weighed heavy on her."

"She had nothing left but your mother," I told him softly. "She was all that was left of her and Silas's love. And you read how you reminded her so much of her sister, Lucille."

Matt walked over, putting his hand on the grave marker beside my own. Poor Lucille. Spirited and brave. Independent and gutsy. She had a job, was happily living with friends, was going to be married, and it all ended in one night. There was so much we'd never know—who Harlen paid to kill her, how the murderer managed to get her to meet him at the Hostenfelder pond. I was a bit surprised that all this hadn't come to light over the years, that Harlen hadn't been black-mailed by the man who'd done the deed, because I was sure he hadn't killed these two people with his own hands.

A man like Harlen Hansen had friends, like a judge and people on the police force. And perhaps he made sure the guy, or guys, he hired to kill Silas and Lucille left town, or died mysteriously themselves.

"It's a sad story, and I don't want to remember my grand-mother as a victim," Matt announced. "She was a kind and honest woman, who was brave and stronger than she thought. She was prepared to give up everything in her life to be with the man she loved, and when she found out she was pregnant, she was ready to face life as a young unwed mother with only her sister to help her. That's brave."

"And in the end, when all her other options had been taken away from her, she did what she needed to do for her child," I added.

Matt slid his hand over to cover mine. "Thank you, Kay. Thank you for being a nosy busybody and bringing all this to light. Now I know just how brave my grandmother really was, and what she was willing to sacrifice for my mom."

And now I had a beautiful piece of dining room furniture without a ghost, and the satisfaction that my nosy busybody self had helped a restless spirit find peace. I pulled my hand out from under Matt's and away from the grave stone, smiling up at him. "Want to grab a quick cup of coffee before I have to go to work?"

He smiled back. "Absolutely. And no matter what you say, I'm calling it a date."

ACKNOWLEDGMENTS

Special thanks to Lyndsey Lewellen for cover design and typography, and to both Erin Zarro and Jennifer Cosham for copyediting.

ABOUT THE AUTHOR

Libby Howard lives in a little house in the woods with her sons and two exuberant bloodhounds. She occasionally knits, occasionally bakes, and occasionally manages to do a load of laundry. Most of her writing is done in a bar where she can combine work with people-watching, a decent micro-brew, and a plate of Old Bay wings.

For more information:
libbyhowardauthor@gmail.com

ALSO BY LIBBY HOWARD

Locust Point Mystery Series:

The Tell All

Junkyard Man

Antique Secrets

Hometown Hero (October 2017)

A Literary Scandal (November 2017)